THE PURPLE SWAMP H

Penelope Lively is an award-winnin                                    era-
ture. She received the Booker Prize                                   aim
for *The Photograph* and *How It All Began.* Lively is a Fellow of the Royal Society
of Literature and a member of PEN and the Society of Authors. In recognition of her contributions to British literature, she has been appointed Dame
Commander of the Order of the British Empire. She lives in London.

www.penelopelively.net

\* \* \*

Praise for *The Purple Swamp Hen and Other Stories*

"On the spectrum of elderly female novelists, Brit division—with twinkly old
dears at one end, as Lively has suggested, and formidable cranks and grandes
dames at the other—she is somewhere in the middle, friendly and polite with
just a hint of steeliness. . . . Lively's productivity has been so steady and relia-
ble that she is sometimes taken a little for granted. In this country she is not
nearly as well-known as she ought to be, and even in her own—although she
has won both the Booker Prize and the Carnegie Medal for children's literature, the equivalent of our Newbery Award—she is not as big a name as, say,
her contemporaries Margaret Drabble or A. S. Byatt. She has a fervent following and regularly sells out at literary festivals, but has remained just on the
edge of the radar. Lively's prose is sharp, precise, perfectly pitched, but shrinks
from flashiness in a way that has sometimes been mistaken for cozy or
middlebrow. . . . By now, though, her body of work proves that certain themes
never go out of fashion: One of her great subjects turns out to be the way the
English middle class, always insecure, is always reinventing itself. . . . Her
books just get crisper and more tightly controlled."

—Charles McGrath, *The New York Times Book Review*

"'The Purple Swamp Hen' is remarkable for its economy and unsentimental
empathy. Nine pages of wry, unsparing narration from an unlikely source
convey the essence of the rich and the enslaved in Roman times. And it establishes a valuable interspecies rapport between an abused servant girl and an
astute wetland bird. The other stories in this satisfying volume center on
humans, and mainly in England. And throughout, Lively deftly and crisply
reveals the challenges and secrets in domestic relationships, as well moral
and emotional qualms and the unexpected arc of unsung individual lives. . . .

So graceful is her prose, so acute her understanding of the 'muddle' of human behavior and emotional chaos beneath British reserve, it is clear this compact format also is Lively's métier. In *The Purple Swamp Hen and Other Stories*, she maps out with clarity an array of marital and intergenerational relations over moments or decades."                    —*The Seattle Times*

"Lively has an impeccable ear. All stories but one are animated by an unflappable omniscient narrator, swimming effortlessly between exterior and interior points of view. Lively is considered a traditional writer, but her unconventional transitions are subtly experimental. . . . Her stories reinvent the world."                    —*San Francisco Chronicle*

"The stories in this jewel box of a collection are ample evidence that age has done nothing to dim the extraordinary talents of its insightful author. . . . Penelope Lively, a keen observer of human behavior, captures with startling precision the essence of what annoys, angers, frustrates, and satisfies the human heart."                    —*Inside Jersey*

"One of the wonderful things about short story collections like Penelope Lively's is their diversity of settings. . . . Lively's writing is poignantly funny, and the theme seems to be one we can all relate to: the existential misunderstanding of one another and the impossibility of changing this fact. Managing to juggle the light and dark as only the most skilled can, Lively's collection is well worth your time and emotions."                    —*Read It Forward*

"How well do we ever know another person? That's the leitmotif of this witty but piercing new collection by Man Booker winner Lively. . . . Even in her darkest tales, Lively's fundamentally serious take on our tangled emotional lives is never bleak, merely ruefully accepting. A treasure trove of fictional gems."                    —*Kirkus Reviews* (starred review)

"Lively struts her stuff in this collection of delectably acerbic and canny short stories. In gin-and-tonic prose, Lively, steeped in history and fluent in English conventions, is keenly forensic when it comes to the nature of hypocrisy and stoicism, secrecy and lies. . . . Lively, perfect for fans of the Margarets Atwood and Drabble, as well as Shirley Jackson, neatly tracks class divides, the fizzling of marriages, and a long-brewing rivalry. Droll fables and mordant ghost stories round out this adroitly wise and mischievous gathering."                    —*Booklist*

"The same measured intelligence and subtle humor that characterizes Lively's novels is present in this story collection. The stories often bear rereading, as Lively's quiet elegance rolls by so smoothly. . . . Effortless and masterly."
—*Publishers Weekly*

"A tour de force . . . Almost twenty years since the publication of her last book of short stories, Lively has rediscovered the form with this superb collection."
—*Financial Times*

"Immensely enjoyable . . . Lively's tone is not elegiac but something far sharper, and she does not twinkle: Lively is not that kind of grandmother. She is funny."
—*The Guardian* (London)

"Thoughtful, intelligent, and light of touch . . . Lively has the gift, rare and wonderful, of being able to peel back the layers one by one and set them before us, translucent and gleaming."
—*Sunday Telegraph* (London)

"Spry and world-wise, 'The Purple Swamp Hen' is an enchanting story that sets the tone for the rest of this stellar collection."
—*The Observer* (London)

"Penelope Lively has guts and style. She takes a situation and holds it upside down, rattling its pockets until she has squeezed out of it every last ounce of meaning and turned the whole story, stylistically, on a sixpence. You are in the hands of a master who can use a shopping trip to explore the whole spectrum of human behavior. Yet there is something unnerving about her ability to see through her protagonists; they get away with nothing, and you, as the reader, feel under scrutiny, too. Here Lively is at her most affecting."
—*Daily Mail* (London)

"These stories continue to explore Lively's obsessions, not only with the mystery of memory, but with the tensions that develop when characters try to sustain a discipline of work while trying to build an intimate life with another person. . . . Her style is a delight."
—*The Irish Times*

# The Purple Swamp Hen
# and Other Stories

## PENELOPE LIVELY

PENGUIN BOOKS

PENGUIN BOOKS

An imprint of Penguin Random House LLC
375 Hudson Street
New York, New York 10014
penguin.com

First published in Great Britain by Fig Tree,
an imprint of Penguin Random House UK, 2016
First published in the United States of America by Viking Penguin,
an imprint of Penguin Random House LLC, 2016
Published in Penguin Books 2018

"Abroad" was published in digital format by Penguin Books in 2013.

ISBN 9780735222038 (hardcover)
ISBN 9780735222052 (paperback)
ISBN 9780735222045 (e-book)

Printed in the United States of America
1   3   5   7   9   10   8   6   4   2

Set in Dante MT

# Contents

# The Purple Swamp Hen
# and Other Stories

# The Purple Swamp Hen

I am the Purple Swamp Hen. *Porphyrio porphyrio*, if you are into taxonomy and Latin binomials. And, let me get this clear, I am *Porphyrio porphyrio porphyrio*, the nominate subspecies, not to be confused with the Australasian lot—*P. p. melanotus*, or the Indonesian crowd—*P. p. pulverulentis*. And others. No, indeed; we are talking species definition here, the enduring stuff, and thus I endure—founding father, the Mediterranean nominate. I am eternally defined, thanks to Linnaeus, himself stuck in the seventeenth century, and we would have been rather beyond his range—we've never bothered with Scandinavia nor indeed with the Americas, they have quite enough species of their own, by all accounts. That said, our range is extensive, and it seems that in conservation terms we are, in a general sense, of Least Concern—in your time, that is. Though I'm glad to say that we—the home team, the Mediterranean Purple Swamp Hen—require strict protection on account of habitat loss, hunting and pesticide use.

Wondering where all this is going? Have patience. You'll get your story. You know me. You know me on the famous garden fresco from Pompeii—somewhat faded, a travesty of my remarkable plumage, but nevertheless a passable portrait. You all exclaim over those frescoes: the blues and greens, the precise depiction of flora and fauna. Oh, look! you cry—there are roses, and ferns, oleanders, poppies, violets. And oh! there's a pigeon, a jay, a swallow, a magpie. You don't cry—oh! a Purple Swamp Hen, because the vast majority of you can't recognize one. You eye me with vague interest, and pass on. It's just like a garden today! you cry.

No, it isn't. Wasn't. I am—was—in this garden because it was a Roman garden and the Romans kept us there for ornamental purposes. Occasionally they ate us, but more often they didn't. We decorated the place, alongside the statues and the fountains. That's one distinction, though the tradition persists, I believe—those creatures called peacocks—but I regard us as unique in terms of horticultural decor. But, make no mistake, the garden of Quintus Pompeius, where I passed my time, was nothing like any garden you've ever known.

It hosted fornication, incest, rape, child abuse, grievous bodily harm—and that's just Quintus Pompeius, his household and his associates. We fauna simply got on with the business of copulation and reproduction; far more imaginative, *Homo sapiens*. The climate of the Bay of Naples was warm (and going to get a lot warmer, but we'll come to that), and they liked to be out of doors as much as possible. Eat out, sleep out, wash the dishes, pluck a pigeon, gossip, quarrel, wallop an old slave, fuck that pretty new one, plot, scheme, bribe, threaten. Get drunk, utter obscenities, vomit in the acanthus.

I saw it all. I heard it all.

Let me fill you in on the general situation that autumn, in the household of Quintus Pompeius. Livia, wife of Q. Pompeius, has a new hairstyle. Major event—oh, yes. Fetching curly strands around the forehead. The new hairstyle is appreciated by Quintus, and even more so by Livia's lover, Marcus Sempronius, business associate of the husband, who does not know of this further family arrangement. Quintus himself is deeply embroiled in politics; he wants to be elected to the city council, to become a magistrate, which means an intensive process of persuasion, bribery, boasting and general manipulation of what passes for democracy in Pompeii. Of his children, his eldest son, Titus, aged eighteen, is theoretically employed in the family winery but spends most of his time hanging out downtown with his friends. His younger sister Sulpicia helps her mother chivy the slaves around. The two youngest children, aged five and six, occupy themselves in the garden—making mud pies, digging for worms, catching grasshoppers, pulling the wings off butterflies. Chasing Purple Swamp Hens.

Quintus and his son Titus both have their way with the new slave girl, Servilia, whenever they feel like it. Nobody would question their right to do so. Servilia is fourteen years old.

Servilia washes dishes. She also sweeps, empties chamber pots, carries water, and is being trained to help Livia with her toilette. She is not as yet very good at this, and gets cuffed a lot.

Other slaves, too, do all these things. The whole place is in a ferment of activity, morning till night, from the fetid stew of the kitchen area to the relative fresh air of the garden. People everywhere—fetching, carrying, getting in each other's way, shouting, being shouted at. The atrium fills up with those who have come to see Quintus Pompeius—to cut a deal with him, get rooked by him, curry favor with him, sign up to some propitious arrangement. He may take a turn in the garden with one or two of these, which is how I knew that he was cornering the market in Etruscan wine imports, that he was spreading salacious rumors about a fellow candidate, that he owed money in various directions and resisted payment, that he was owed in various other directions—and was uttering dire threats.

Thus, the daily life of the household. And of scores of other households in the city—prosperous households, the households that called the shots. Elsewhere, much the same took place, on a lesser scale—among those engaged in selling bread and oil and grain and fruit and fish and meat and dormice and sea urchins. Plus the provision of various services, including of course sex. Not so much garden life, there; horticulture the preserve of the well heeled.

All the same to me—master, mistress, slave. Egalitarian—my

outlook. Detached, you might say. A forensic interest in the practices of this curious species.

Let us take some instances of attitude and behavior.

They find it perfectly acceptable that one lot possesses another lot. So, half the inhabitants of the city wait upon the other half; a section of them are commodities, to be bought and sold like a loaf of bread or a flagon of wine.

*We*—we swamp hens, swallows, golden orioles, sparrows and all else—eat in order to survive. No more and no less. They eat to excess, with deplorable consequences. Eating as entertainment it would appear to be. Along with the lavish consumption of wine, which has this humiliating effect on them. Except that they apparently find it enjoyable rather than humiliating.

Quintus Pompeius is a wine magnate. Was, was . . . I keep forgetting. Preserved into your time on that fresco, floating timeless, I have somewhat lost my grip on chronology. Quintus P. is ashes now, or rather, he is a featureless gray cast, stared at by innumerable visitors to the site of his demise.

My demise also? Certainly not. Wait. We'll get to that.

The Q. Pompeius wine business is both manufacture and distribution. It procures grapes, it processes them, stores the product and then enables inhabitants of the city to get legless as often as they wish or can afford to do so. An ideal trade—the bottom is never going to fall out of wine. The human race is fueled by it, one observes.

This, then, was the setup: the family, the household, the supporting business. All coasting along as normal in the run-up to that climacteric event of which you already know.

Livia took an almighty risk. She entertained her lover, Marcus Sempronius, in a secluded part of the garden while Quintus Pompeius was out of the way, visiting a political supporter. Entertainment in every sense of the word; I heard the moans and groans and passed by with disdain.

Sulpicia, her daughter, was courting the son of a neighbor. They too made full use of the garden. Lucius, a Greek slave who was the principal cook, was engaged in a feud with Sextus, the Libyan thug responsible for janitor duties; these two brawled outside the kitchen, where Servilia scoured pans and occasionally fetched up as collateral damage.

Servilia is of interest. She was a recent acquisition, spotted by Quintus P. and bought off a friend, for whom she was surplus goods. I am no connoisseur of the human female but it would seem that she was appealing. Other males of the household eyed her up, but were wise enough not to encroach. As far as I was concerned, she was just another presence, until a particular morning which made her of interest.

The children had been chasing me. This happened, not infrequently. I kept well away, when they were in the garden, and if they did get near and start molesting, I am quick on my feet and could be off pretty smartly. On this occasion, I was unwary. They crept up, and the boy had me by the neck.

"Pull its feathers off!"

"Kill it!"

"Let me have it!"

They squabbled. I lost a tail feather.

"I saw it first! I want it!"

"Kill it! Let's kill it!"

She must have heard, Servilia. She came over. She remonstrated. She said that their parents might not wish me killed. The children told her to get lost.

And then she reached out, prized me out of the boy's hands, and let me go.

I flew up onto the fountain.

We looked at each other, bird and girl.

"Thanks," I said.

"My pleasure," said she.

No language passed, but perfect understanding. Something I had not come across before with that species.

The children rushed off to their mother, and reported Servilia for un-slavelike conduct. Livia was not much interested, preoccupied with a fear that Quintus might be on to her activities with his associate. Also, a swamp hen is garden decor, nothing like as valuable as a Herm or a statue of Bacchus, but still worth preserving. We are not that fecund. We don't breed easily. My mate and I had not done well that year; two eggs addled, the surviving chick picked off by a cat.

My mate? Oh, yes. Have I not mentioned her?

This happened a few days before the event, the final hours. During which time things warmed up in various ways at the villa of Quintus Pompeius. Never exactly a haven of tranquillity, it became the scene of violence and recrimination.

The Greek cook and the Libyan thug had an almighty dustup, as a result of which the thug suffered a black eye, and the cook several broken ribs, which put paid to cooking duties for the time being. A thug is always replaceable, but a good cook is an essential commodity, so the thug got a further pasting, by order of Quintus P.

The carcass of a kid destined for a banquet disappeared from the kitchen. Other culinary material had gone missing before and it was suspected that an assistant cook, another recently acquired young slave, was purveying goods to an associate in the city. He was questioned, with some brutality, and accused the guard dog, occasionally let off its leash. Since it was not feasible to question the guard dog, the slave was further interrogated and eventually admitted guilt. He was beaten and dispatched to the slave market.

A couple of days later the banquet took place, replacement kid or kids having been acquired, along with much else. The whole place reeked of cooking, slaves rushed about sweeping and scrubbing, the couches in the triclinium were laid out with covers and cushions. I knew what we were in for—a raucous evening, inescapable because the triclinium gives on to the garden so that even if one roosted at the farthest corner, the noise could not be avoided nor, indeed, the occasional guest coming out for a breath of fresh air or a quick vomit.

And so it was. Lamps lit everywhere, night turned into day. Slaves staggering to and fro with dish after dish, wine poured and poured and poured again. Talk, shouts, boisterous laughter. Now and then someone burst into song. Eventually I gave up any attempt to roost and took up a position in a clump of irises beside the path. Various bits and pieces were falling from the dishes that came from the kitchen, some of which were tasty.

Thus it was that I observed the furtive meeting between Livia and her lover Marcus, both of them taking temporary absence from the gathering on some pretext. A passionate embrace behind the fountain, noted by me, and, unfortunately, by Quintus Pompeius who had also risen, in order to give directions to the slave in charge of wine supply.

He saw. They knew that he saw.

Nothing said. Not then.

Later, much was said. A short while later, when the guests had dispersed. Marcus Sempronius was one of the first to leave, looking preoccupied. My guess is that he was to find that various useful arrangements with Quintus P. were now history. What passed between Quintus and his wife was audible throughout the villa, for some while. He roared; she bleated excuses. He clouted her; she shrieked. Slaves lurked nearby, interested and appreciative. The children woke up and wailed. The guard dog barked. It was nearly dawn before the place quietened down. Then swallows dipped into the fountain, the golden oriole began its song—somewhat repetitive, I've always thought, but preferable to human cacophony.

That evening reverberated, over the next few days. Quintus Pompeius was now in a thoroughly bad temper, which meant that everyone had to watch their step. Those seeking his attention in the atrium found him terse, dismissive, intolerant. Any slave who put a foot wrong got biffed. Those who didn't got shouted at anyway. The children, bouncing up to him, discovered that he didn't like children anymore. Livia cowered in the cubiculum.

A bad atmosphere then, at the Villa Pompeius. A presage of things to come? They might well have thought so; a credulous lot, the human race. If there were some propitiatory sacrifices, some attempt to pacify the gods, I was not aware.

The first earthquake came at midday. Not a particularly strong one—a mere shudder by comparison with some. A garden Herm fell over—hideous head of Hercules—some kitchen crockery was smashed. People exclaimed—a bit of shouting, but not much excitement. Earthquakes are not uncommon here. This one did not cause undue alarm and it was soon over.

And then another, two days later. Longer, stronger. Rather more comment this time; the gods are angry, they said to one another—or, more practically, better stand clear of the building till it's over.

I do not like earthquakes. We do not like earthquakes—swallow, dove, oriole, sparrow, and rat, mouse, cat, dog, the animal kingdom. An earthquake makes you uneasy, restive. The stability of things has been questioned, in every way.

We ride them out, usually. Take cover. Batten down till it's done.

This was different. I knew. I knew when I felt that second heave, that ripple of the earth beneath my feet. The acanthus wildly waving. Bricks tumbling from a wall. I knew that this would end, but was also a beginning. Something more would happen.

I spoke. We can be noisy, we swamp hens, when it is appropriate. We can be loud. I called my mate. Come, I said. Out, out, out.

I was near the kitchen, where also was Servilia. I flew up onto a wall. My mate joined me.

"Go!" I said to Servilia. "Get away from here. Just go. Go, go, go."

Bird to girl. Again. She looked at me. She heard. She understood.

I saw her put down the dish she was scouring, look around, get to her feet. I did not wait. We're off, I said to my mate. Now. We flew.

We circled the city. I needed to get my bearings, see which way to go.

We flew. Fast. Low. And, as we flew, I saw a great black cloud had risen above the mountain, a cloud like some immense pine tree reaching up into the sky.

We flew higher, above the city, up and beyond. The air was thick, stuff falling from above. And there was movement now below, people on the road, carts, horses, people leaving the city.

I saw a girl running. Away from the mountain, away from that black cloud. Running, running.

On that day, of all days, there would be no attention paid to a runaway slave. May she have run far.

As we flew. Far, far. Away from the mountain, until there was no more falling stuff, and that terrible black cloud was distant. And then, at last, in a good marshy place, where there was no garden, no fountain, no presiding Herms, but water, reeds, the kind of habitat appropriate to *Porphyrio porphyrio*, we came to earth again. And there we settled, and bred, as have my descendants, thus ensuring the survival of the species from that benighted age into your own. Where things are done differently, but it is not for me to proclaim progress, or otherwise.

# Abroad

Fifty years ago there were peasants in Europe. France was full of them—Spain, Portugal. Greece had the very best—prototype peasants. As for Macedonia, places like that—you were spoiled for choice. Plowing with oxen and a sort of prehistoric plow. Heaving water out of wells, carrying it picturesquely on the head in a pitcher. Washing their clothes in the river, drying them in colorful swathes on the banks. Driving their donkeys to market, with interesting goods in panniers. Small boys herding goats on rocky hillsides. Women hoeing fields. Old men grinding maize. Landscapes peppered with peasants, doing what peasants do, wearing proper peasant clothes—women in long skirts and aprons, men with black waistcoats and baggy trousers.

In England we didn't have peasants. Just the rural working class. Farmworkers. Not the same. Not colorful, not picturesque. They had tractors and mains water. They dressed from the Co-Op.

We were artists. Tony and I. We needed subject matter. We needed arresting, evocative subject matter. So we needed Abroad. Anyone artistic needed Abroad in the 1950s. You needed the Mediterranean, and fishing boats pulled up on sandy shores. Olive groves under blue skies. Romanesque churches. Market squares with campanile and peasantry. Sunflowers, cactuses, prickly pears, cypresses, palms. We needed scenery; we needed well-furnished scenery. Particularly we needed peasants. Real, earthy, traditional peasants.

I sketched. Tony both sketched and photographed. A sketch would be worked up later into an oil painting, back home. The photos were prompts, reminders; that girl with the great load of washing on her head could be used in due course—such a graceful stance.

Abroad was cheap—relatively cheap. We were skint, and you could potter around Spain or Greece for weeks on a few pesetas or drachma or whatever. One was always in a muddle with the money—what this scruffy note was worth, or this fistful of coins—and then pleasantly surprised when some old dear was apparently offering B and B for tuppence ha'penny, or so it seemed. Mind, not B and B as we think of it; more like a bare room with an iron bedstead and a jug and basin, and some crusty bread and coffee in the morning. But all so authentic. We wouldn't have gone near a hotel or a *pension*, even if we could have afforded it. We wanted to be seeing things as they saw them—the locals. I've still got a sketch I did of one of those old dears—all in black, head to toe, brown wrinkly face, and so grateful for whatever we paid. Portuguese, I think. Or possibly Italian. Or was that in Yugoslavia?

We were young—early twenties. We'd met at art college, set up together, decided to get Abroad, as much as possible, for as long as possible. Abroad then was just Europe; now it's everywhere—Sri Lanka, Thailand, Barbados, wherever. But in the 50s Abroad meant the Continent, and that was that.

Tony was so good-looking. Those sort of rather ravaged good looks, even at twenty-two or so—thin face, dark brown eyes, dark brown hair flopping over his forehead, dark brown body too because we were so much in the sun. Abroad's lovely sun. And he was very much the artist: French beret, check shirt with the sleeves rolled up, linen slacks.

And me? I was pretty arty too, back then. Jeans, when jeans were hardly known. Bra top, bare midriff. Sloppy Joe sweater when chilly, fair hair to my shoulders, tied back with a pink cotton hanky. The hair is neither long nor fair these days. Went mouse, then gray, and shoulder length won't do at eighty. Oh, well; I dare say Tony has worn a bit, too. Wherever he is. If he still is.

Attractive? Yes. I was. We were a somewhat arresting couple, I'd say. Sketching away in little Greek fishing villages or beside some Spanish field, with the fishermen heaving nets or whatever, and Spanish peasants picking and cutting and digging and generally getting into nice poses that you could quickly rough out for future use. There'd be plenty of banter directed at us, that of course we couldn't understand, all perfectly amiable, and lots of smiles and flashing white teeth as well. Peasants always seemed to have rather good teeth. Except for the old ones. Shortage of teeth, then. Thank heaven for modern dentistry. Mine aren't too bad.

Mind, we did sometimes realize that we weren't seeing things as the locals saw them. There was the day of the life class. Somewhere in France. Tony had decided he wanted to do some life drawing. We were in the depths of the countryside, we had had a picnic by a field. "Come on," he said. "Life class." So I had stripped off and I was sitting there, posing and sunbathing both at once, and Tony had his sketch pad out, when all of a sudden this—well, peasant—appeared. The farmer, I suppose. And roared at us. Shouted and yelled. And then stormed off, and next thing a couple of gendarmes arrived. I'd got my clothes on by then. So we were down at the police station explaining for hours. No charges, but don't do it again.

There could be problems about money, too. Peasants seemed to be overconcerned with money. All that careful counting out of coins, in the markets; endless bargaining over the equivalent of a farthing or two. Goodness, farthings . . . I've almost forgotten them—odd that the word swims up. We always got the coins confused. If you accidentally gave too little there'd be an end to the flashing white smiles and a flood of abuse instead. Not so picturesque, suddenly. You learned to tread carefully, where money was concerned; a bit of an obsession, apparently, in those circles.

We weren't having to worry about money all that much. Everything so cheap. We could eke out what we'd brought for weeks on end, and if we found we had absolutely miscalculated, or we wanted to stay longer, well—there could always be an emergency telegram home. Mummy and Daddy would come up with something—grumbling a bit. I was supposed to be on an allowance, and not overspend, and they were a tad tight-lipped about Tony, and us not being married, or even thinking of it, but they were in favor of Abroad. Mummy felt it was so educational. So if we ran short it would just be a question of a post office, and an arrangement with some bank, when we'd found one. Not all that thick on the ground, often, banks; peasants seem to do without them.

I shouldn't keep saying peasants. Sounds patronizing. People. Country people. Thing is, they were—in a way that doesn't exist anymore. No peasants in Europe now. I know—I've been there. No long skirts, black waistcoats, oxen, prehistoric plows. Banks all over the place. I don't know where young artists are to go nowadays.

Right—people. Peasant being merely a technical term. Nicely different people, which was what we liked about them, apart from the subject potential. Not boring English. England was so boring in the 1950s. Everyone agreed about that, even Mummy and Daddy. They went Abroad as much as they could, too, though a different Abroad from ours: Italian Riviera, and French châteaux. You didn't holiday in Wales or Cornwall, in the 1950s— not if you could possibly help it.

Not boring English, and not speaking English. That was part of the appeal—not knowing what people were talking about. Just that chatter of Spanish or Greek or whatever. You were on the outside, not involved, just looking on, which is what you were there for. We had a bit of French, from school, but that didn't get you far. Peasant French was something else. Sorry—country people French.

Goodness—how we got around. It amazes me, now, looking back. We never cared for being stuck in one place, so it would be into the car and off—when the car was behaving, that was. Old Hillman. Ancient Hillman—proper old banger. Many punctures, many stops while the radiator boiled. Many failures to start unless pushed. Places like Greece and Yugoslavia, we used buses; elsewhere, the car. Blissfully empty roads—you tootled along on your own, deep in France or Italy or wherever. A few of those old Citroëns—*deux chevaux*—the occasional pickup truck, lots of bikes. Garages as infrequent as banks, which could be a problem when the Hillman was playing up, or when we'd forgotten to get petrol. You always carried a can, in case.

But the point was to be carefree, independent. Artists can't be hampered by the *dailiness* of ordinary life—Tony felt strongly about that. Doing the same things each day, forever bothered about money. Art has to be freed from all that. Everything was very *daily*, in Europe, back then—daily life was what we were looking at constantly, what we were sketching. Subject matter, said Tony, that's the point. He was very serious about his work—more experimental than I was, more abstract, very much a colorist. He had tremendous promise—everyone said so. He was going to be the next Graham Sutherland, Paul Nash. I think it hasn't worked out like that. I'd have heard.

We weren't getting on quite so well that summer. We disagreed in Brittany, argued our way down to the Auvergne, made it up somewhere around the Pyrenees, squabbled again in Catalonia. Issues about where to go next, and how long to stay here or there, plus the Hillman was being really tricky. I said I was tired of Spain. Tony said we've hardly *touched* Spain—amazing landscapes, super people, so *visual*.

The last time he'd say *that*.

Actually, we were on good terms, the day we came across the wedding party. We'd driven deep into the back of beyond, miles from any town, hardly any villages even, just isolated farms, fields of this and that, hillsides with goats. So I had laughed and agreed. Only problem was the Hillman, which kept coughing and spluttering and stalling. We stopped, to give the tiresome thing a rest, and did some sketching beside a pasture with cows wearing bells, got the car started again, with difficulty, and then a mile or so further on suddenly there were all these people.

A farmhouse, and a long table outside with eats and drinks, and this party going on—everyone done up to the nines, and the younger ones dancing, and the bride and groom very obvious. She was about my age—Spanishly gorgeous, long black hair, glittering eyes.

We slowed down. Slow was all the Hillman cared to do at that point, anyway. But we were both thinking the same thing . . . must draw this. Tony was reaching for his sketch pad before he was out of the car.

We stopped a little way away. Tried to be unobtrusive. Sat on a stone wall by the road. Did quick sketches: that old fellow at the end of the table, the woman pouring wine, those girls dancing.

Unobtrusive? Two people couldn't turn up in a car out of nowhere without being noticed. Children came over, peeked at our sketches, ran back giggling. A woman brought two glasses of wine, indicated that we could join the party.

We did. We went and sat by the table, accepted a bite of this, a taste of that, sketched some more. Big smiles all round.

What luck! The real thing, so authentic.

Tony drew the bride. He was good at a likeness; she came out well. Much approval—laughter, and the sketch passed from hand to hand.

*Artista?*

Yes, we said. Yes. *Artista.*

*Bueno! Muy bueno!*

Then the bride's mother wanted her portrait done. And a sister. Tony obliged, though I could see he was getting a bit bored with this. It was like being one of those people who sit around at Piccadilly Circus with an easel, doing bespoke likenesses. Not his scene.

After a couple of hours we decided to move on. You can have enough of authentic, eventually. So lots of smiles and handshaking, and we headed back to the car.

It wouldn't start. Ignition dead. Terminally dead.

Our situation had been observed. Some of the men came over and set about giving us a push.

That usually did the trick. Not this time.

Somebody opened up the bonnet, peered inside. Much tutting and frowning. Others looked, expressed dismay.

Garage? we said. *El garage?*

Laughter. Gesticulations. We got the message. The nearest garage was twenty-five kilometers away.

The father of the bride had taken over a leadership role. The farmer, evidently. Big, burly man with a forthright manner. Some sort of conference took place—everyone talking at once—and then he seemed to be offering a plan. He gestured toward the old pickup parked by the farm, one of the only two vehicles in sight. The other was a battered little car that didn't look any healthier than ours. The means of transport around here was evident: mule, cart, and bike.

Some rope was fetched. The idea, it seemed, was to tow the Hillman to this distant garage.

We beamed. *Gracias, gracias.*

A pause. Unmistakable indication of what was needed. *Dinero. Peseta.* Money.

Ah, we said. *Sí, sí.*

Trouble was, we were pretty well out of cash. Not a long-term problem—we had traveler's checks. But we'd been meaning to find a bank for the last couple of days, and then never did.

We got this across. *Banco,* we said. We get to a *banco* and then we have *dinero.* No problem.

Yes, problem. Money up front. Surprising how clearly the farmer got that across.

Oh, come on, said Tony. Surely they can trust us? When the car's fixed we get to a bank, and bring him what's needed. We go with the bloke in the pickup and then stay with the car till it's done.

He explained, all smiles. Pointed to car, to pickup, indicating time on his watch. "Then—*banco!* Then—come back here! *Aquí! Dinero!*" He displayed our traveler's checks, which provoked derision.

No. No and no. *Aquí.* Stay here.

The pickup had been driven up and the Hillman roped behind. Tony sighed: "Well, if that's the way they want it. How long's this garage going to need, I wonder?"

*El garage? Cuanto tiempo?*

Much shrugging and rolling of eyes. You were talking days, several days. A week.

By now we were getting a bit fed up. Evidently we were going to spend rather more time with authentic Spanish country life than we'd reckoned with. And the warmth had rather gone out of our welcome. Treatment had become distinctly brisk. Do this, come over here. We got our stuff out of the car, as indicated, watched the Hillman bump away behind the pickup, carried the haversacks, easels, sketchbooks, painting equipment over to a barn where, the farmer's wife proposed, we should sleep. Hay bales. Chickens for company. Oh, well. We'd have a tale to tell, at least.

The farmer was taking a thoughtful interest in our paints. Picking up tubes of color, fingering brushes. He looked at Tony, with a sort of smile. Speculative smile.

"*Artista. Bueno!*"

He beckoned. We followed him into the big farmhouse kitchen. Flagged floor. Huge old black stove. Whitewashed walls. To which he pointed. Then to himself, to his wife, to others who had now crowded in.

"*Niente dinero—pintura.*"

"Oh, for heaven's sake!" said Tony.

This, it seemed, was the deal. You haven't got any cash to pay up front for taking your car twenty-five kilometers to the garage, getting it fixed, and bringing it back, so you can pay in kind. A nice fresco on our kitchen wall—group portrait of the family. Take it or leave it—except that leave it wasn't an option.

Tony painted all through the next day. He painted the farmer, as central figure. He painted the wife, alongside. He painted the bride, who had gone to live just a couple of fields away, it turned out. He painted the bride's two little sisters.

There was criticism, at points. The farmer wanted his money's worth. This face not so good, do it again. More color here. Put the family dog in there.

Tony painted on, the following day. The son. An old granny, brought in for the occasion on a cart. A couple of aunts.

"It's like the Last Supper," he said. "And I'm not bloody Leonardo, am I?"

He was given a glass of wine, presumably to keep his strength up. Food was provided twice a day; basic food—coarse bread, soup, bit of hard cheese, a chunk of sausage, a tomato. Authentic, you had to call it. Same as they were eating themselves.

And me? I was not painting—oh, no. I had been measured as

an *artista*, it appeared, and found wanting. There were other plans for me.

I fetched water. The well was some way away from the house. You pumped with a sort of iron handle thing. It made your arm ache. Then you carried the buckets. I hadn't known before that water is *heavy*. Several trips, over the course of the day. *"Bueno,"* said the farmer's wife. I suppose she did this, normally.

I made use of the water, as instructed. I washed clothes, in a tub. Scrub. Scrub some more. Rinse. Hang out to dry.

*Bueno, bueno.* And here's another lot. Do those now. When you've fetched more water.

The kitchen floor. Scrub again. On hands and knees. I scrubbed around Tony's feet, as he worked. I said, "What if we just refuse? Say we're damn well not going on like this."

"He'll just say—OK, push off, get lost. We're miles from any-where. We haven't got the foggiest idea where they've taken the car."

I said, "We haven't been very clever, have we?"

Tony stared at his fresco, teeth clenched.

"And you've got the best of it," I said. "At least you're painting. Just try doing this."

"Frankly," he said, "I never want to bloody paint again."

*"Ándale!"* snorted the elderly uncle who was posing for his place in the lineup. Irritable interjection—get on with it.

On the third day I went out into the fields with the bride's sisters. We were on weeding duty. Stuff growing; you weeded everything that wasn't the right stuff. Bent double. Back ach-ing. Hot. The girls chattered and laughed. I didn't.

Everybody was being perfectly nice to us, but brisk. Firm. Our position was made quite clear. You have to earn your keep. Pay for the trouble we've taken.

*El garage?* we said, glumly. *El auto? Cuanto tiempo?*

Shrugs. Three more days, maybe. Four? Five? The farmer's

son, driver of the pickup, who had taken the Hillman to the garage, indicated difficulties. Much trouble, many problems.

After weeding duty came . . . more weeding duty. Different stuff growing in another field. Again, weed everything not the right stuff. When finished weeding—fetch water. And—oh, *bueno*, if you've got nothing to do now you could clean and chop these vegetables for the soup.

I said to Tony, "I told you we'd had enough of Spain. We should have ditched the Hillman and gone to Greece."

"Right now, I'd rather like to go to Brighton."

His fresco now covered most of their kitchen wall, a study of the extended family. People had been brought in by the day, not a second cousin left unturned. Now, it seemed, they had run through the lot. Not the end of Tony's work, though, as the farmer indicated. Backdrop required. Put in the farm buildings—here, see? Behind, like this. And animals—cow, goat. *Bueno, bella pintura*. He had taken to standing over Tony, observing every brushstroke, expressing approval—or not.

I learned how to pluck a chicken. Ugh. The chicken was a treat for Sunday lunch, a scrawny thing. It served ten people. You didn't get much chicken.

*El garage? El auto?* Pathetic, we were.

*Pronto, pronto.*

I had blisters on my hands. Hoeing, that was. Hours of it, where they grew their vegetables. And sore knees. At night, on the hay bales, we bickered.

"If you'd listened to me, we'd be in Greece now."

"I kept saying—look, we really should find a bank before we go any further."

"You didn't."

"I damn well did."

*"Artista!"* I said. It sounded like a term of abuse.

He sighed. "Let's not fight. Sorry."

"OK. Sorry."

We made it up, observed by the chickens.

Another day.

And another, on which there was activity. A man stopped by, driving a battered lorry. Who had, it seemed, some message for the farmer. Long exchange, much bonhomie. The man departed. Discussion between farmer and son. Uncles appear, and join in. Finally, we are summoned.

*El auto—terminado!* The car is ready. Everyone most genial— smiles all round, as though this were a personal achievement.

Great! we say. Fantastic!

*Vámanos*, then.

We were to be taken in the pickup by the son. We collected our stuff, said our good-byes. Long spiel from the farmer's wife, amiable but with, you felt, a bite there. You may have learned a thing or two, was the gist of it, I think.

Gracious farewell to Tony from the farmer, as from a patron who might well provide a reference, if required. Tony took a photo of the fresco. Black and white, of course, in those days, and it came out very murky, when we had it developed. I wonder if he's still got it.

We drove to the village where the garage was, bumping around in the pickup. And there, indeed, was the Hillman, now viable, as was demonstrated. Starting up without protest, engine running nicely. Two new tires.

The bill.

Ah. Of course, we said. *Sí, sí.*

The pickup and its driver had departed. Whatever made us think the garage repair bill might have been covered by our labors at the farm?

We produced the traveler's checks, with brave confidence. *El banco?* Looking around, cheerfully, as though there might be one just over there, by the grocery store and the homely bar.

A stony glance at the checks, from the mechanic. *Banco?* What *banco? Dinero, por favor.*

It came to both of us that life might be about to become even more daily than it had just been. We looked at each other. A fresco on that whitewashed wall at the back of the garage? Nice portrayal of truck, pickup, old car or two?

And me? Heave tires around, like that boy over there? Wash forecourt. Wash trucks.

"No," I said.

Negotiation, we realized. There was a way. *Where* was there a bank?

Twenty kilometers, it emerged, eventually, in the nearest town. And yes, all right, the mechanic would come with us in the Hillman, we would cash our check, pay him, and return him to the garage. The bill to be adjusted to take his time into account.

And so it was. On the way, this man became rather more amiable. He had noticed our painting equipment in the back of the car.

"*Artista?*" he inquired.

We said that, yes, we were indeed *artista*.

He laughed. Continued, after a moment: "*Dinero?*" Laughing again.

Much money in that, is there?

No, said Tony. *Niente dinero*. At least—*poco dinero*. So far.

The mechanic gave him a friendly slap on the shoulder. Amuse yourself then, mate.

We arrived at the bank, paid off the mechanic, returned him to his garage.

I don't know if we were both thinking the same thing. We never really discussed it. The trip rather disintegrated after that. We headed for Portugal, but it had lost its charm; we found we didn't any longer much care for rural life, and made for cities. Tony suddenly found street scenes inspiring.

I was thinking about money, and how one had somehow underrated it. I thought about peasants—sorry—counting out every coin in those markets. Stronger stuff than I had thought, money.

Back in England, we sort of drifted apart. I haven't heard of Tony in years.

I've carried on painting, of course. Clive has always made a point of saying, "My wife's an artist, you know." There's a cachet, no question. He brings home a packet, as a barrister, so it's been neither here nor there if I sell things or not—we don't need the money. I'm glad I realized when I was young that actually money signifies. I've been able to—well, organize my life so much better.

# The Row

They had had a row. A long-drawn-out, well-nurtured Sunday row. It began in the kitchen, over breakfast, a slow simmer coming to the boil, and then it flamed further, up in the bedroom, she making the bed, he looking for a clean shirt. It subsided, sank to embers, but then, downstairs, later, they blew on these and up it came again nicely, flaring here and there every few minutes, words muttered, spat out, hurled from room to room: "You always . . ." "Don't tell me you . . ." "And another thing . . ."

She couldn't think why she was married to him. What had possessed her? The world is full of men—men of every size, shape, persuasion, clever men, funny men, charming, potentially devoted men, men who would put the rubbish out without being asked, men who would fix a dripping tap, ravishingly handsome men who would send you weak at the knees, calm authoritative men you could rely on in a crisis, men destined to become prime minister who would attribute all their achievements to one's support and sacrifice, men who would forgo anything in order to foster one's own glittering career, men who didn't sing out of tune in the shower, men who picked up their socks, men who cooked and washed up after.

Some of the men she had missed out on gleamed at her, almost perceptible—a smile of invitation, conspiratorial glances.

All those . . . Any of those . . . And she had *him*.

It is called pair-bonding. Animals do it. It is a universal compulsion to shack up with someone else, something else. Birds do it, bees do it, even educated fleas do it. We do it, for better or for worse. Oh, big laugh—that ironic choice. Chuntered out by goofy vicar at our wedding, glasses slipping down his nose all the time and then he'd hunch them up, and my new shoes were killing me, big mistake, those Manolos, two hundred quid and never worn again.

Pair-bonding is for reproductive purposes, in animals. We just do it for the sake of it, many of us. We ourselves have not reproduced, David and I, we are not even considering reproducing at the moment and right now the reproductive act is out of the question. Yuck.

You shack up at that time of life when everyone else is shacking up. So, inevitably, you shack up with one of those in sight and available at the particular moment. Instead of the myriad others that are not. Human pair-bonding is about as considered, as deliberate, as the pair-bonding of seagulls or termites or whatever. Actually, termites breed in colonies, don't they? So not appropriate. Equivalent of Mormons, or some oriental harem. But point being that pair-bonding, shacking up, is essentially driven by circumstance.

She considered her own circumstances, back then. She had probably known about eighty to a hundred men around the right age. Subtract those that were gay or married. Still leaves quite a few; you lost some as others laid claim to them, but more would have hove on the scene. So there was a choice, but derisory choice when set against general male potential. She might just have been allocated an unpromising pool.

Pond. Puddle. And she had fetched up with *him*.

At lunchtime the row could have dwindled to sullen ashes had he not mentioned that he would be away next weekend. Boys' jaunt with old college friend: have a go at rock climbing.

At once, a whoosh of flame from those embers. "And when do I . . ." Back to business, all guns firing.

She knew that particular old college friend, and didn't care for him. A blokey type, a man's man, a "meet you down the pub" man. She couldn't remember if he was married or not. Poor her, if he was.

Online dating vastly expands the availability pond, of course. It becomes an ocean, indeed. She knew one or two people who had tried it, but did not report favorably. One said it was exhausting and most of the men were suspect in some way; she had settled for a friend of her brother's in the end, whom she'd known for years. Another had had a bad experience in a taxi, and was trying to sue the website. No, online dating was somehow artificial, it flew in the face of nature, you didn't want to go there. Have been there.

Nature? But it's nature that serves up the whole situation. The compulsion to pair-bond, shack up, build a nest, get a mortgage, go to Ikea, get self-assembly this and flat-pack that, end up paying a man to assemble and unflatten, blame each other, have first row, second row, third row, become row proficient.

Did she and David have rows pre-marriage? In courtship days, in early living-together days? Amiable spats, she seemed to remember, rather than your full-scale practiced row. And back then there was the satisfaction of having made a choice, settled for this particular man. He had novelty appeal; if there were shortcomings you were happy to overlook them, you were in this new place, coupledom.

Coupled. Coupled in conflict, today. Together in adversity. Upstairs and downstairs, with breaks for rest and recuperation. Rancor filled the house—a sour miasma. The house, the home, the three-bed semi in Plumstead freighted with its enormous mortgage, filled with his things and her things and their things—the house, the home, the hearth.

The cage, she thought, today. The Sartrean hell in which we snarl at each other and I don't know why I'm here rather than in all the other places I might be with all the other men there might have been. Beckoning homesteads scrolled before her eyes like estate agents' advertisements: Cornish cottage by the sea, Cotswold manor, New York brownstone, hacienda, villa, château, old Provençal *mas*. The men too, except that they were less defined, a shadowy elusive crew, mere suggestions of intriguing otherness, the ones you would never know.

Instead of the one you know inside out, in sickness and in health, in bed and out of bed, in love once and in whatever it is that one is in today. Some maddened mutation of love.

What's he doing now? Banging about in the garden shed.

Oh, he's going to cut the grass. Which he does only when in a temper. Something satisfying about hurling a machine up and down, it seems.

Grass. It occurred to her that grass had assisted their first meeting. Not cutting it—sitting on it. She traveled back to that moment: there is she, sprawled on the grass at the edge of a village green, cricket match going on—thwack-thwack—and there is he, sitting down alongside, saying, "It's a bit damp, isn't it?," gallantly offering her his jacket as rug. If she hadn't gone to stay with her friend Sophy that weekend at Sophy's parents' home she would never have fetched up at a cricket match, cricket matches so very much not her thing, have never watched one since. And if she had not gracefully accepted the jacket, and it turned out that he'd known Sophy from primary school days and was working in London now and she would meet up with him again at a party Sophy gave a few weeks later.

If I had not gone to that party, if I'd had flu, broken a leg . . . If I had not known Sophy, indeed, and that was because of working with her at that bookshop and striking up a friendship. Any of those ifs, and I wouldn't have met him at all, instead I'd have met . . .

One of those shadowy others. The might-have-beens.

Whoosh, whoosh—the rhythmic surge of the mower, now. It should be soothing. Is not.

Everything he does is abrasive, today. His very presence is abrasive. That presence she once had longed for, counted the days until, reveled in.

I mean, for heaven's sake, one was in meltdown, waiting for phone calls, messages. Nothing else mattered, the rest of life pushed aside, on hold.

She thinks of this, returns to this person she once was.

That first time we went out, after he'd talked more to me than to anyone, at Sophy's party. Tate Modern, lunch, a walk by the river. Degree of meltdown, already. Couldn't stop looking at him.

It's a form of insanity, isn't it? Mental derangement. You have lost control, your life is no longer your own—in service to emotion, expectation.

First time we kissed. Outside that flat I was sharing. In the rain. Standing on the step, rain on our faces. For weeks after that, months, rain made me think of it.

First time we went to bed. Oh. Oh, oh.

All those first times. It's this process of discovery, isn't it? The exploration of a someone else, full of surprises. Ah, he loves opera, like me. He doesn't like curry—fine, nor do I, from now on. He votes Lib Dem, he drives rather fast, he's queasy about spiders, he's got a mole on his left shoulder, he plays a mean game of Scrabble, he gets hay fever, he has read *Ulysses*.

Eventually you run out. You aren't surprised. You begin to know what he will say, do.

So? That's no big deal, is it?

Well, familiarity breeds . . . No, it doesn't. Shouldn't.

He's going to slam the mower up into the shed now, come out, walk back across the lawn, our little pocket handkerchief lawn, march into the kitchen through the back door, carefully not looking over at me, here on the patio reading my book.

All that time we didn't have a mower and a minuscule lawn

and a patio and all these accessories to marital gracious living. The time in that poky one-bedroom flat, meaning flat with one and a half rooms, kitchenette and bath.

She thinks of that time.

Me learning how to cook. Well, both of us, but me becoming best at it, so we tacitly agree that I am principal cook. He is euphoric about my chicken chasseur and we have this joke that he only married me for gastronomic satisfaction.

He is in perpetual negotiation with the bossy bloke on the ground floor about David leaving his bike in the communal hallway. We call him the Gauleiter and conspire to think up suitable propitiatory offerings: a cactus, a jar of sauerkraut, a henbane plant.

Time of constriction, frustration. Well, no, it doesn't seem to be, when summoned up, when subjected to forensic gaze.

Then me getting the BBC job and at almost the same time he is promoted and suddenly we have quite a lot more money and after a while it is good-bye to the flat and here we are as snug as you like in suburban bliss.

The pad, the nest, the cave.

Sound of kettle being filled, from the kitchen. He is making himself tea.

She unfurled that whole length of time, from the cricket match till February this year when the purchase was completed and they owned a house and a mortgage, the marriage officially consummated. She homed in on specific points, for further inspection. Our wedding, and never mind the goofy vicar and my stupid shoes, there was that moment looking at each other when he put the ring on my finger. When we did that walk by the sea, and he said, "Come on, quick . . ." Has anyone else ever made love on a June morning in a hidden-away grassy bowl beside the Underhill walk at Lyme Regis? When we drove back from seeing my parents, down the M1 through the night, the new *Carmen* CD on full blast, singing along. When we had that weekend in Bruges and saw those paintings through exactly the same eyes—aesthetic empathy. When I broke my toe and he did everything for us both, when we climbed Skiddaw and hugged each other at the top of the world. When he was knocked off his bike and they called me from A & E and for one hideous moment I thought he . . . When he brought a huge bunch of peonies for my birthday—last year, was it? Or the year before. Oh, he'll remember.

But I can't ask him. We're having a row.

It occurred to her that he too had all this in the head, every moment of it, but differently skewed, his view not hers, and that was interesting in itself, all those moments twice preserved. How different were they? Could you, together, unpick each and identify where you saw the same and where you didn't? Plump out a memory, as it were; give it, for each, a further dimension.

That's the thing, isn't it, she thought, you're so bound up with someone else that you share time itself, you have whole chunks of time in common. But then there's a whole lot more that isn't— all of him before we met, all of me. Time now when we're not together.

Him in the kitchen. Me out here. Oh, but here he comes.

He asks if she would like tea.

She indicates that she might.

You are no longer just you, she thinks. You are you and him. Not entirely, oh no, but a whole slice of you is that. I am the me who goes to work every day, is there, working, is maybe with a friend for lunch, maybe goes out on my own of an evening. And there is the me who is doing what he does: living here, eating, talking, reading, watching the telly. Going to bed.

She accepts a mug of tea.

And this is the most provocative situation, is it not? It invites abuse, manipulation, tyranny, subjection. A person is supposed to accommodate herself—himself—absolutely to another person. It is unnatural. OK, but it's nature that sets it up in the first place. Of course, of course.

It is unnatural and provocative and precarious and challenging. It demands forbearance and stamina and abnormal powers of empathy and perception.

It is also . . . And yes, it is also all those other things. The opposite. The converse. The place you want to be.

She has drunk the tea. She picks up the empty mug and goes into the kitchen.

Where he sits, also with empty mug.

He says, "I'm sorry if you are."

Later, much later, in bed, they lie shoulder to shoulder, punch-drunk, played out, replete. Like those stone figures in churches, she thinks, the knight and his lady, together forever and always, and that would be just fine. The peonies were last year, he has confirmed, and he asks if she would like sunflowers this year, or orchids, or maybe a magnolia tree.

In the darkness, at the edge of the room, a few of those might-have-been men have dared to hover, that shadowy crew.

You'll be lucky, she tells them. Get lost.

# Who Do You Think You Were?

In west Somerset in 1787 a young woman who could not read or write, but knew fine how to skin a rabbit or pluck a fowl, forged her way through autumn mud from Rodhuish to Withycombe, where she would fetch the old red rooster from her aunt Mary Ann. The rooster was destined for the pot, and has no further part in this story, except that as it was handed over, squawking, both Sarah and her aunt experienced a most unusual sensation, like a mild electric shock (a concept that would have baffled them).

Aunt Mary Ann said, "A goose walked over my grave."

Sarah was busy subduing the rooster, and tucking it under one arm. In her other hand she carried the basket that had contained a fresh loaf and some potatoes, fair exchange for the rooster. She shivered, though she hadn't been feeling cold, and said she'd be off back, there was rain to come. The rooster made one final protest, Aunt Mary Ann went into her cottage, and Sarah Webber walked on into the rest of her life.

*

In London in 2015 another young woman stares at a screen. She scrolls through names, a cascade of names; she frowns, she taps, she pulls up a further name torrent. She makes a note on a pad beside her laptop. She scrolls again, and lo! she spots a most satisfactory connection. She pounces, makes a further note, and then she decides to call it a day. She closes the laptop. She is twenty-four years old, and is engaged in postgraduate work; she would be hard put to it to pluck a fowl, let alone skin a rabbit.

Caroline puts the laptop into her briefcase, the laptop that knows everything, or most things, and in which the past is stored, by way of a thousand names, tens of thousands of names, hundreds of thousands. The laptop knew about the relationship between Mary Ann Crowhurst and Sarah Webber, though possibly not about the red rooster.

It is the end of the working day, for Caroline Gladwell. She works in the Reading Room of the British Library, because she may have need of its resources, though much of the time she is making use of the omniscient laptop. She is doing an MA in Economic History, of which a component part is the dissertation on a subject of her own choice. She has chosen to research her own family history, back to the early seventeenth century, in order to demonstrate the directive force of economic circumstance on individual lives. She will show why unemployment in the shipbuilding industry impelled this ancestor to leave Portsmouth, why opportunities in domestic service brought that one to Cheltenham. At the moment she is tracing forebears of her mother's, who appear to have been stuck generations deep in the West Country, being born, marrying, dying, within a relatively small area. Agricultural laborers for the most part, and it would seem that conditions were favorable enough to allow of staying put.

Caroline is pleased with her choice of subject for the dissertation which, she feels, lends color to the sometimes gray backcloth of economic history. Persons, people—the real people who are the drivers, the facilitators, often the victims, of economic developments. Names—she can cite them—the Johns and Georges and Alberts, the Elizas and Alices and Janes—whose toil has contributed to a climate of prosperity, or otherwise. She will pinpoint certain names, evoke their circumstances, and tether them with a detailed account of their particular occupation—the dissertation will be richly informative about bricklaying, needle making, baking, brewing and much else. It will bring the past alive—make it relevant.

Caroline is intensely concerned with history—she is hoping for a career in academic life—and she sometimes feels that the past is seen simply as an object of study, that its very reality is ignored, the fact that it happened, that these people lived and died. The populace within the laptop.

Next year Caroline will get married. Caroline Gladwell will become Caroline Fox, though of course she will not use Alan's name, generally speaking, but will remain Caroline Gladwell. In this she is very different from the young women whose names have scrolled down in front of her, and for whom marriage meant immediate abandonment of their birth name. They became their husband's appendage, forever after. A change that is a signifier for the times, she thinks, as she gets a number seventy-three bus to head for home. Our times. Now, which is so much not then.

Home is a one-bedroom flat in Stoke Newington, for which Caroline and Alan pay a wicked amount of rent. The flat is the ground floor of an insignificant two-story Victorian terrace house which would once have housed a lower-middle-class family of modest means, and is now worth around a million pounds. If Caroline and Alan were to buy their flat from the landlord they would have to pay half a million or so for sitting room, bathroom, bedroom, kitchen, broom cupboard and minuscule entrance hall; that is of course out of the question.

Alan is quite favorably placed in economic terms. He is on the lowest rung of the civil service ladder, at the Home Office. If he beavers away for the requisite number of years, and climbs accordingly, he will eventually be in a position to hang his hat on a pension. Caroline herself has no such certainty, not yet, but with her MA under the belt, to add polish to her First, she will be equipped for a decently paid teaching job, even if she doesn't make academia.

The flat feels chilly; it is November. The days are closing in.

Caroline puts the heating on, draws curtains, unpacks the shopping she picked up on the way. Lemon garlic roasted chicken thighs for supper.

Over which, presently, she and Alan exchange their days. He has had a slight run-in with a superior, and would have liked to give him a piece of his mind, but was sensible enough not to do so. Alan is pragmatic, clever, and usually cheerful; he is stockily built, has large and compelling brown eyes, and Caroline loves him inordinately.

She tells him about today's search. "And then suddenly everything clicked into place. I realized that a Mary Ann Crowhurst was the aunt of a Sarah Webber, and I could fit that family tree together."

"Your Somerset peasants?" says Alan.

"Agricultural workers."

"Hodge," says Alan. "The generic term for nineteenth-century laborers. No names, just a tribe of Hodges." He too read history at the university, and has acquired arcane pieces of information.

"And that's what I'm doing," says Caroline triumphantly. "Filling in the names."

They smile fondly at each other across the lemon garlic chicken. Alan is thinking that Caroline's face is a perfect heart shape, and that it is quite unfair for a girl to be so pretty and also so bright. Caroline is savoring the moment; if she were a cat she would be purring.

Caroline says, "It is almost creepy that these people are my forebears. That there's a *connection*. Genes. DNA. And that nobody, so far as I know, has ever done this before. Reached back, and made the links. Touched them, as it were. I am their future." She was silent for a moment. "It feels quite odd. You identify, almost."

"You can't really identify. It's impossible. Their circumstances are so different. The mind-set—the assumptions, the

expectations. Think of it—the age before antibiotics, sanitation—
people likely to be clobbered by anything and everything."

She stared at him. "All the same . . ."

"And," he went on, "most appropriately—it's that program
tonight. Do you want to see it?"

Alan is referring to the television program *Who Do You Think
You Are?*, in which some celebrity is confronted with their family
history, usually to be startled by the revelation of an ancestral
convict, or slave owner. Reality genealogy.

And so, later, they watch with amusement as a well-known
actor learns that his great-great-great-grandfather was impris-
oned for body snatching. As compensation, there is another
distant grandparent who died in the workhouse. Penury is
always a badge of honor.

"They didn't get that from the parish records," says Alan.
"The body snatcher."

"No, of course not. They have to investigate further if someone looks interesting. As do I."

Indeed. When Caroline can identify a name that invites
inquiry—on account perhaps of their trade, or their sudden
movement from one place to another, or even an early death—
she tries to acquire further information. This is where she may
have to leave her comfort zone in the British Library Reading
Room, and hive off in pursuit of unfamiliar archives. She may
try to find a particular street, even a house, a gravestone. Actually, all this is quite good fun—heading off to places she has
never been to before, engaging with helpful people in some
archive, taking to unfamiliar streets and spotting survivals.
Oh—here's the terrace in which so-and-so lived, still standing,
no longer a slum, all gentrified now. And yes, here is the gravestone I'm after, giving substance to a name on a list. She really
did live and die.

At the moment Caroline is in pursuit of a descendant of those

West Country Hodges/peasants/agricultural workers, a man who seems to have broken out and headed off to Bath. Why? What was he doing there? Did he marry, have children?

*

In Bath in 1840 a young man worked on a building site. A railway station was being built, though the young man was barely aware of the ultimate purpose of his labors. Suffice it that he had daily work, and daily pay—superior to the circumstances he had known where he was born and grew up, where there might be work, and a meal on the table, but very well might not. Today, he would be called an economic migrant, though he has migrated merely across a county.

He is in fine fettle, on this spring morning, heaving barrow loads of golden Bath stone, and thinking of his Eliza, to whom he was married only yesterday. He thinks of the moment when the priest declared them man and wife, when he experienced what felt like a great surge of being—an affirmation of his very existence. And he thought of what Eliza said, after: "I came over all funny, Tom, when he said that—'man and wife.'" And he had known that she must have shared this momentary euphoria. Eliza is Bath born and bred; her father is an innkeeper, and Tom and Eliza have rooms over the inn, where, in due course, they too will breed.

*

In London in 2015 Caroline Gladwell spots a marriage entry that homes in on her wandering Hodge and most satisfactorily establishes that, in 1840, he was married in Bath to Eliza Fulbrook. She places Tom and Eliza at the head of a new family tree, in expectation of the births for which she will search in due course. Caroline suspects that Tom had been drawn to Bath by the work opportunities offered in the construction industry—Brunel's new railway station for instance—and she will now do some research on that. She thinks of this as coloring in—giving background, substance, to the stark recital of names. A name can then bloom a little—it can conjure up the image of a person: Tom Webber can become a robust young man laboring amid the dust and clamor of a nineteenth-century building enterprise.

Caroline thinks a lot about age—ages—as she pursues one name and another. Infant mortality, early deaths, the relative rarity of those who make it into their eighties. Death hovered, two hundred years ago, even one hundred years ago. Caroline has four octogenarian grandparents, doing quite nicely, bar various hip or knee problems.

Caroline herself is young, in today's terms. But would have been seen, more, as mature, a couple of hundred years ago—a hundred, even. Perceptions of age shift, as expectation of life lengthens. One third of the children born today will live to be a hundred.

My own, perhaps, she thinks. Goodness! Disappearing off into the twenty-second century. She and Alan plan to start a baby in a year or so, after their spring wedding. Another signifier for the times, she reflects (scrolling through some Bath births of the 1840s, in search of Tom Webber's progeny)—child born untypically in wedlock, when actually, nowadays, most are not. And born according to schedule (all being well . . . ) instead of arbitrary, possibly unwelcome.

Ah! She has found it—a son born to Tom and Eliza in 1841. Within wedlock, by a comfortable few months.

Caroline now accelerates the nineteenth century. She whisks through time, disposing of decade after decade, until in due course she has nailed down the descendants of Tom and Eliza Webber, unto the fourth and fifth generation, forging ahead into a new century. Not her mother's direct ancestors, but a branch line and interesting in itself for economic flexibility; male

Webbers abandon the building trade and become grocers, brewers, and in one instance a funeral director.

But at lunchtime Caroline closes her laptop, consigns the past to another day, and steps out into the present, away from the British Library and in the direction of Oxford Street. She's taking an afternoon off; she has a date with a friend, to consider wedding dresses. Rosie is also getting married next year. Weddings are almost a cult, for their generation. People marry with a flourish, in their late twenties or so, often having been together for several years.

Caroline remarks on this to Rosie, as they inspect an acreage of white and ivory silk, tulle, organza, in the bridal department.

"Why do we do it? My mum says in her day most of her friends just sneaked into a registry office, and then had a family lunch somewhere. She and my father didn't bother till I was nearly two."

"My parents never have." Rosie works in a bookshop, would like to get into publishing. She is short and dark, a foil to tall fair Caroline. "What about this one? Too frothy for me."

"I don't want froth either. So why do we?"

"Because each other does, I suppose. I've been to five this year already. You've got to retaliate. This one?"

"No—I don't want to look half naked. My parents were still in recovery, I imagine—my mum had nearly died."

"Having you?"

"Yes. Everything went horribly wrong. First I was stuck, and then she had a hemorrhage. And infection too—she was very ill after."

"Scary . . . Mostly it seems to be a doddle, nowadays. Sue Parker—remember Sue?—she went shopping in Brent Cross the next day. This?" Rosie brandishes a beaded confection.

"You're joking . . . Utterly bling."

They are getting tired of wedding dresses, and retreat to the coffee shop.

"I'm saturated in marriages," says Caroline. "Researching. Marriage after marriage. But it's just names and dates. You want to know more. What did she wear? I had a great-great-great-someone or other yesterday in Bath. Eliza. You find yourself imagining them."

"Write a historical novel. Be the next Hilary Mantel. Cutting-edge stuff nowadays."

Caroline shrugs. "I can't think like that." She wants to explain that what she reads in lists, entries, bare references, has come to reflect some alternative reality. Nothing to do with fiction. But it would be hard to put into words without sounding fey, and in any case Rosie has moved on to other matters: a flat she and her partner covet but cannot afford, a job interview next week, the person they caught nicking books in the shop. "Actually, in a way, I couldn't help feeling—good on him. More high-minded than your run-of-the-mill shoplifter."

They consider this ethical point over another coffee, and part company. Having got nowhere with the matter of wedding dresses, as Rosie observes.

"Perhaps we don't take marriage seriously enough," says Caroline. "An excuse for an event, rather than a rite of passage."

They agree to pillage the wedding department at Selfridges, on some other occasion.

Somewhere in London, in 1821, a young woman is giving birth. She is in the final stages of labor, but the child is awkwardly placed. It (she, as it happens) is presenting feet first; the labor has been arrested, hour by hour, the woman is weakening, dying. Eventually the midwife decides to risk manual extraction, plunging her hand into the uterus to grasp the child by the feet and pull—a procedure potentially harmful to both mother and child, but needs must, in this instance.

The child is dragged forth. Wonderfully, she cries. The mother is beyond speech or crying. And the placenta has not been delivered. The doctor, summoned earlier, now arrives, late, hurrying in from the busy street, and at once rummages for the placenta.

Two days later, Maria Gladwell dies.

*

Elsewhere in London, in 2015, Caroline arrives back at the flat later than usual, and voluble about her day's work.

"I got so involved today. Guess what—I've found myself, as it were! Caroline Gladwell. How weird is that?"

Alan considers that it is not all that weird. Caroline was, after all, a popular name in the 1820s. Caroline—his Caroline—has explained that she was now pursuing her father's ancestry, and had arrived at this woman, a Maria Gladwell, who died in childbirth in 1821, the child, Caroline, having survived.

"I suppose so. But it did rather jump out at me. And the mother dying."

"But your mother didn't," says Alan.

"Only because of twentieth-century obstetrics."

Caroline had decided to follow up that entry in the family tree with a short discursion on the conditions of childbirth in the late eighteenth and early nineteenth centuries. She has already read fairly extensively. In the early 1800s, she has learned, one in eight childbirths ended with the death of the mother. Maria Gladwell was one of those, then: a statistic.

The entry that Caroline had found stated only that she died in childbirth—which had led her to the confirming entry of the birth of her daughter Caroline two days earlier. What happened in the interim? Well, Caroline speculated, Maria had very likely contracted puerperal fever, in the absence of basic hygiene—the notion of hand washing in a solution of chlorinated lime was not introduced until the 1840s. And many things could have gone wrong during the birth, which would nowadays be addressed by a forceps delivery, or an emergency Cesarean. Or, if the child was known to be awkwardly positioned, a Cesarean would have taken place automatically.

"She died," Caroline continues, "because she was giving birth in 1821 and not, like my mother, in 1991."

"And what happened to your namesake?"

"That's what I must find out."

Finding her own name had startled Caroline rather more than she admitted. Your name is your identity. She had thought about this, coming home on the bus. I know who I am because I know my name. I don't know who these people all around me are because I don't know their names. You read of people who have forgotten their name because of accident, or illness, and they are displaced, adrift, in need of help. The medics come running. You are not allowed to be without a name. Your name confirms that you exist, that you are you, that you can stand up and be counted.

And she had my name, back then.

Of course there are always people who have the same name as someone else, thousands of them. There are no doubt other Caroline Gladwells today—I may have walked past one in the street. And that feels a bit funny, too. But somehow not as weird—disturbing, even—as a person dead a long time ago.

How did she live? Marriage? Children? When did she die?

There is a new flavor now to this piece of research, Caroline finds. This oddly personal element. A kind of fortuitous intimacy. She is both intrigued by this and a bit disconcerted. Wrong-footed, as it were, as though the great neutral resource into which she taps had suddenly answered back. Spoken.

She gets down to it the next day. She has sited this Caroline within a new family tree. The interesting thing will be to see if she is a direct forebear, to find her children, and theirs, and see if they can be fined down to a great-grandparent, say.

First, she needs a marriage. But can find none. Oh.

So . . . To the deaths. And then she has it.

Caroline Gladwell died in 1847, aged twenty-four.

Twenty-four.

The rest is stark. An instance of the bald entry that sometimes accounts for a death that is out of the ordinary.

"Struck by a coach."

Caroline stares at this. Around her, the Reading Room is going about its business, impervious, while the screen in front of her delivers its news.

Struck by a coach. Killed.

It occurs to Caroline that this could indeed have been news at the time. The search does not take long. Sure enough, in an issue of a London paper a few days later than the death date, there is the item: ". . . tragic accident . . . death of a young woman . . . stepped into the path of an oncoming coach . . . onlooker who rushed to try to pull her back said she appeared distracted, perhaps unwell . . . coachman much distressed."

Caroline reads this. Once. Twice. The brief item is somehow resonant. She reads it yet again. She wants at once to tell Alan about this. Twenty-four. How weird indeed . . . She starts a search through the other London papers of the period for further coverage, but finds none, and as she does so, she begins to feel—well, rather ill. Shaky. Not herself at all. Flu or something coming on. Oh, I really don't feel too good.

She decides to go home—it is gone five, anyway. She gathers up her things, and leaves the Library. She crosses the open space outside in the darkening early evening, heads for the bus stop, and then feels really quite dizzy. Taxi, she thinks, taxi for once— I'm just not well.

She stands on the pavement, searching the pounding traffic for a free taxi. Stands with aching head, feeling quite unsteady. Traffic roars past, buses surging down the bus lane, steady stream beyond. Oh, to get home. Oh, taxi, please. And there at last is the orange light she needs, free taxi, out in the traffic, about to go past.

She steps from the pavement, waving. And as she does so everything happens at once: she is hearing horses' hooves, thundering hooves, but it is a seventy-three bus that she has not seen, that is almost on her, and in that instant arms have grabbed her by the shoulders, someone is pulling her back, the hooves are fading, she is hearing the screech of brakes, she is back on the pavement, a man has her by the arm—a burly, efficient man saying, "You all right? You bloody nearly . . ."

"I'm all right," she says. "This time I'm all right. This time. Thank you."

# Old as the Hills

Here she is. Stick. Which I don't need yet. That patrician way of surveying a room—she hasn't seen me. I shan't wave. Let her find me. She's worn well—oh, yes. Apart from the stick. Doesn't look eighty. Do I? She's not done up, but understated stylish. Good coat, arresting scarf. Neat hair—all over silver gray, not pepper and salt like mine. No glasses—surely she used to? Oh, she'll have had the cataract op.

*

*You are in my head, Celia. Multiple versions. Multiple Celias. Is this one the first time I set eyes on you? If so—or if not—I still am. Still seeing you across a different room. Blue dress, summery blue, talking to . . . oh, I've no idea who. Laughing. And then you look over toward us, you smile. At Hugh, I later realize. Much later. And you wander over to us, still smiling, and it seems that you and Hugh have met before. "Celia," he says to me. "Celia Binns." A name I'll get to know. The blue dress has a crisp white collar, a nipped-in waist. You are slim, at thirty-six.*

*

Not now. She is a touch overweight, I'm glad to see. Snap.

Ah, she's seen me. The stick raised a little, in recognition. Faintest of smiles.

She approaches. Slow, with entitlement, forging through the tables. People looking up as she passes. She knocks someone's jacket off the back of his chair; he leaps up—apologizing, by the look of it. Of course—not her fault.

And here she is.

"Jane!"

Yes, I am Jane. I know that. "Hello, Celia."

"I haven't been to this place before." She is removing her coat; a waitress materializes at once, to take it, pull out her chair, flourish a napkin across her knees.

I say that I have been here once. It had seemed all right. She has settled in, is considering me. She is thinking that I look all of eighty, that I have jowls, pouchy eyes, that I ain't what I used to be.

Or maybe she isn't. She says, at once, "So you decided to miss the funeral. Delicacy?"

"Norovirus," I say. Which is the truth. She can believe it, or not—her choice.

"Ours all sat together. People thought that was so nice."

Ours. My children, her child—his children. My grandchildren, her grandchildren—his grandchildren.

"Quite a lineup. The youngest ones behaved impeccably. My Sophie. And that small lad of yours." She picks up the menu. "I shall probably go for something salady. Not a great eater, these days."

Grief? Or concern about obesity? Not that she is anywhere near obese. Just rather stout, like me.

We choose. We order. We refuse wine (did I see her hesitate for a moment?) and sip mineral water. I ask if she is going to stay in that house. That large, expensive house.

"Of course. Why wouldn't I? All our things . . . I'd hate to part with anything. And so many memories." A little sigh.

Indeed. We all have those.

"Dear me," she says. "Long time since we saw each other, Jane. Maisie's wedding?"

I correct her. Another funeral, which I did attend.

"Oh yes—his mother. I'd forgotten you came. Good of you, considering. I'm sure Hugh appreciated that."

★

*Oh, he did. If an air of deep embarrassment and confusion equals appreciation.*

*There he is, and why am I surprised that he is older, has some gray hair, a different face. Me too. And you, Celia, and you. Elegant in black, neither embarrassed nor confused. Running things. Meeting and greeting. Presiding over the funeral bakemeats.*

*You are sixty. As am I. Well into middle age, and you carry it off well. As a successful gallery owner should. I am successful too, in my own sphere, but university administrator is less conspicuous.*

*You have forgotten, you say (you say . . .), but I have not. I am there still in some stratum of the mind, supported by my Maisie, my Ben, observing your Toby, screwing myself up for strained exchange with Hugh. Observing Hugh.*

*You stand in gracious conversation with some elderly relative and remain thus in my head, competing with this subsequent Celia, Celia now, Celia seated, eating salade niçoise.*

*

"Not before time, one felt," says Celia. "But perhaps you got on better with her than I did."

I am noncommittal. Actually, I had problems too. Seems we have that in common.

"Odd to think she wasn't much older than we are now. But there it is. We're as old as the hills, aren't we?" She grimaces.

Old as the hills. And young as all those other Janes and Celias that crowd the mind. And Hugh. And Hugh.

*

*He cannot bring himself to say it. He has to bring himself to say it. Long ago. And now. Now and forever.*

*"Jane," he says. "Jane, I've got to tell you . . ."*

*And I know. He need not bother.*

*"Celia Binns," I say.*

*

"One never thought it would happen, old age," says Celia. She is tucking into the salade niçoise, I note. "Just something that happened to other people." She laughs. "You were more realistic, I imagine."

"I tend to be realistic," I say. "Something I've learned."

She gives me a sharp look. Wonders if I am making a point. Well, yes, Celia.

"One can only try to make the best of it, I suppose. The occasional treat. I'm going on a little cruise next month. Hugh and I had planned to do that at some point." She sighs again.

I am impassive.

"He was so stoical. Right to the end. I know you'd want to hear that."

Would I? But impassive seems inappropriate here. I nod.

"Treats," says Celia. "And physiotherapy. I have a wonderful physio. But maybe you're in better nick than I am. I'll have to have a hip done."

I mention my torn shoulder tendon, to keep abreast of her. Celia says she believes the best shoulder man is at the Royal Free. A friend of hers went to him.

"You know," she says, "I'd go back to the forties, if I could have my time again. Forget youth—nothing but Sturm und Drang. The forties were good. Fifties not at all bad, either."

*

*Celia at fifty. Yes, that memory slide comes up at once: Celia at my Ben's wedding, her hat trouncing all other hats, being tactfully unobtrusive but nevertheless emphatically there, impossible to miss. Hugh and Celia. Celia and Hugh. I am used to that, by now, but forever not. It is always an affront. So at my son's wedding I am affronted.*

*

"Eighties are an outrage," says Celia. "What have we done to deserve this?"

I do not care for this implied community. I say that as far as I am concerned we are rather lucky to be living where and when we do and thus to have got to be eighty at all.

Celia pulls a face. "Lucky? I don't feel particularly lucky."

I regret the word. Not quite what I meant. I say so. "Statistically lucky," I say.

She laughs. "Well, I don't feel like a statistic either. Just myself in a condition that I never anticipated." She puts down her knife and fork; she has demolished the salade niçoise. "And usually the oldest person in the room. Though not right now—there's a real old codger over there. Ninety if a day. Boring the socks off his granddaughter, by the look of it. That's what one is afraid of. Boring the socks off. Are you bored, Jane?" That smile. The Celia smile.

I am not bored, oh no. I do not return the smile (who could compete?), but ask after her grandchild (his grandchild) Sophie, who has had health problems. I am not, as it happens, particularly concerned about Sophie, but one should observe the proprieties.

Sophie is much better, it seems. "And, incidentally," says Celia. "I imagine you've had the lawyer's letter. About the legacies. Same for all of them."

I have. I say that my Ben will be glad of his—he is in his first job, low paid, and saving for a car.

"Oh, that rings a bell. Being young and strapped for cash. I remember being twenty-one and lusting—*lusting*—after a dress I couldn't possibly afford."

No image surges forth. I did not know Celia at twenty-one. Nor did Hugh. She would hove upon the scene all in good time. Bad time, you could say.

"Did you get it?" I ask.

"Oh, yes. I found a way." She laughs.

Of course.

The waitress is wondering if we would like desserts. Celia says she could manage something if I would join her. We opt for the lemon cheesecake.

And then . . . "Why am I here?" says Celia. "Surely not for the pleasure of my company?"

I have been waiting for this.

"Satisfaction," I say.

Celia considers me. "Handbags at dawn? Isn't it a bit late for that?"

The pleasantries are done. This is more like it.

"Why Hugh?"

"Well," she says. "Why not Hugh? I was high and dry—my previous attachment had foundered. There had to be someone."

"Someone else's husband."

"Unfortunately. But not entirely unusual, Jane. And he could have resisted."

Indeed, indeed. Point taken, Celia.

"And you thought—Jane will get over it, people do."

She inclines her head: possible agreement. "You found your Chris before too long, after all."

Indeed, again. Quick on her feet, Celia. Level pegging at the moment, it would seem.

"I always liked Chris," says Celia thoughtfully. "Hugh didn't, for some reason."

I am rather pleased to hear that. Affinity would not have done. But this is beside the point.

"How is he?" says Celia. "You should bring him over one day, now that . . ."

Oh no. Oh no, Celia.

"He has sciatica and a prostate problem," I say.

A moue of sympathy from Celia. She will not press the invitation.

Back to business. "No compunction at all?"

Celia reflects. "Well, not really, I'm afraid. After all, I was in love," she adds sweetly.

Oh, come on. "Of course," I say. "Which explains everything."

Celia sighs. "Jane—it's history, all this."

I say that I have always thought history to be of great relevance.

"Oh, I can't think like you," says Celia. "You're so well educated."

The waitress appears. Would we like coffee?

Celia would kill for a coffee, it seems. So would I, I find.

After a moment, Celia says, "Am I supposed to say I'm sorry?"

I have considered this. "No, because you're not, so it wouldn't mean anything."

"Then . . . Satisfaction?"

I tell her that perhaps confrontation would be a better word. "It's called the elephant in the room nowadays. What is never spoken of. Forty-two years ago you helped yourself to my husband."

Celia gazes at me. "Absolutely. I can't deny that. Not an unprecedented situation, but I can see you feel that is irrelevant." She wears a benign smile, but her eyes are steely. It is each for herself now.

And that is fine by me. This has been a long time coming. Forty-two years. I have plenty to say.

So has she.

We get down to it. At last.

Our coffee comes. The waitress hopes we have enjoyed our meal. The restaurant is emptying. People are getting up, putting coats on, passing our table with an indulgent glance and smile: two elderly friends lunching, having a chat about old times. Bless.

# A Biography

TALBOT, Lavinia, aged 70. Emeritus Professor of History, Temple College, University of London. Wife of Professor Gerald Plant. Died suddenly on 18 March 2012. A memorial event will be held in London.

*

Interview with Alice Hobbs. Roundhay Farm, Okehampton. May 4th 2014.

Well, she was always just *there*, for me. Sort of elemental, like weather. And she could be quite elemental, Lavinia—when she was in a mood. Central, always, in the family. But, look, I adored her—absolutely. She was what she was, and what she was, was Lavinia. Rather wonderful. Whatever anyone else says. And people will . . . well, people will say all sorts of things to you. I mean, I suppose you're going to be talking to various people?

Yes, I see. Yes, of course you must. Just, I mean, not everyone . . . But basically Lavinia was—well, unique, wasn't she? I know she could be . . . no one's perfect, are they? There'll be things said . . . I hope you won't . . . Well, you'll balance it all up, I imagine, what you hear, what you discover—not that there is anything to *discover*. A sort of all-round view, I suppose. But I do feel I . . . well, her *sister*.

When we were children? Five-year gap, so that did mean she was always very much the big one. Older, cleverer, could do things I couldn't. I seemed to be forever running after her, about thirty feet behind. Saying, "Oh, Lavinia, *please*, me too . . ." She wasn't unkind, dismissive, ever. Sometimes she'd include me, but she was off on business of her own. Like for the rest of her life.

Yes, we always *saw* each other. When she could manage. But I mean my life was so different from hers—just being a mum for years, and down in Devon, miles from her, and then my ordinary little jobs—the library, helping at the old people's home. The other end of the spectrum from her. She sort of shot on and up and I could hardly believe it was my sister—seeing reviews of her books, and hearing her on the radio. Those TV programs. I was so proud—I'd name-drop her, I'm afraid: "Oh yes, that's my sister."

Yes, she visited. Not that often—but when she could. She'd come for Christmas occasionally. I think she quite liked that— full-on family Christmas. And she'd got less—elemental—by then. She never had those hissy fits like when she was a child. She was much easier to get on with—for me, for everyone, I imagine. But she was always this strong presence. Always some- how the center—if Lavinia was in the room things sort of eddied round her.

Gerald? Oh no, he never came to our place. I hardly ever met Gerald. Nor did my husband. I mean, did Gerald ever step out- side a library, and Sam was a *fruit farmer*. Chalk and cheese.

Happy . . . Well, why wouldn't she be? Her career went rather splendidly well, didn't it? I know she had a few problems— differences with other people at her London job, and she told me there was carping about her television work. They were jeal- ous probably, weren't they? And she and Gerald—well, he did seem rather stiff, I do admit, but I imagine they rubbed along all right really. Oh, I'm sure she was happy. Mostly, anyway.

Look, let me get us some tea.

*And I need to get away from you before I say something I don't mean to, don't intend to, mustn't say.*

*Take a deep breath. Kettle on, warm the pot, get milk out.*

Yes, actually I'd *rather* go back to our childhood. After all, that's when I knew her best. I remember the later part most, when I was—oh, nine, ten—and she was a teenager. Except there weren't teenagers then, they hadn't been invented—people that age were just in a sort of limbo, waiting to be grown up. But Lavinia somehow refused that, she was very much established, very much already a person, helping Mum out at family gatherings—our mother was lovely, of course, but she wasn't an organizer, things could fall apart, and Lavinia would step in and see the table got laid and the food got served, all that. And she wasn't shy, like I was, she could find something to say to grown-ups, carry on a conversation. Goodness, I remember her with Uncle Harry, our cousin Barbara's father, holding her own like anything in an argument about—oh, something political, I think. And he got all ruffled—she was getting the better of him maybe—and told her she was still wet behind the ears. She made that into a great joke, after—always saying, "I must be careful to dry my ears if Uncle Harry's going to be here."

She didn't get her own way, exactly, in the family. No, it was more that she'd decide something and Mum and Dad would go along with it because it seemed the right thing anyway. Applying to Cambridge. Mum thought that was amazing—she hadn't been to university, of course—and Dad was, well, impressed, I suppose. Mum was always a bit—in awe of her, almost.

Me? Oh, definitely. But in a nice way, don't get me wrong. I thought the world of her. There she was, always top in everything at school—smashing to look at too. I mean, who wouldn't want a big sister like that?

Well, I suppose you *could* be jealous but I wasn't. I knew I couldn't be like that in a million years, and that was neither here nor there. And she never treated me as anything but myself—not as someone less clever or less competent. Younger, yes. I was younger. But she'd explain things to me. Tell me what she thought about things.

Bought me a lipstick when Mum said I mustn't have one yet.

Read *Middlemarch* to me and I couldn't understand a word but never mind.

Went round and tore a strip off that girl next door when she'd said I was fat.

Look, do you know, I'm finding this a bit sort of . . . upsetting. Talking about her like this. Do you mind if we . . .

Yes. Yes, do get back to me if you need to.

⋆

Interview with Barbara Stone. University Women's Club. June 10th 2014.

First cousins, yes. And of an age—Lavinia was not quite a year older than me. Can't say we were close at all—you'd meet up at family gatherings and that was about it. In later life I never saw much of her—weddings and funerals only. But she was quite—prominent—when we were both young. I mean, you sort of saw in child Lavinia what she was going to be. The determination, the application. A certain ruthlessness. She ran rings round her parents. Aunt Susan was totally incompetent, and Lavinia would just elbow her aside: "Leave it to me, Mum, *please*." No attribution here, mind you. I don't want Alice wailing that I've been trashing her sister. And she lorded it over Alice. I don't know how the child put up with it.

Assertive—that was Lavinia. At fourteen or whatever. My father got enraged with her, one Boxing Day lunch: "Trying to tell me what was what about Labour party policy. The impertinence." He never forgot—turned the television off when my mother wanted to watch those programs of hers.

I find it odd to think of a book about her. Biography. Well, obviously you . . . no criticism meant, obviously you see her rather differently. Public figure, that sort of thing. You were forever hearing her name. Something to do with the British Museum, wasn't she? Always on the *Today* program. I'm quite aware she was pretty well known. I've never read any of her books.

Oh, are they? Well, I've always read novels more, if anything. You don't get a lot of time for reading—four children and a job in school administration. I dare say Lavinia wouldn't have had such a starry career if lumbered with a family. I was offered something that was a step up, and then the twins struck. After that it began to be too late . . . Irrelevant, so far as you're concerned, I know. Back to Lavinia. I may not have read her books but I did watch that series—*The Child in History*, wasn't that it? History can leave me cold but we're all interested in children, aren't we? At least, those of us who've had them.

You haven't? Well, think twice. Anyway, I did watch, despite there being so much of Lavinia holding forth. It was interesting, I'll give you that. At least we treat them rather better now. And don't have so many. At least, some don't.

Seen as what? Oh—innovative. Was it? Well, I wouldn't know—I don't watch much of that kind of thing. It did get her talked about, I remember. And after that you were always hearing her on the radio. Here we go again, I used to think.

No, no contact really, by then. Alice always sent a Christmas card, but not Lavinia. Just funerals, and there was a rash of those—her parents, mine. She did turn up—quite a performance— very noticeable, kissing all round. Outdressing everyone. She looked particularly amazing in a big black hat, with that hair. I take it you never actually saw her?

Just photos. And the series. Yes, well, that gives some idea. But Lavinia in person . . . Right from age about thirteen, managing to look elegant in school uniform. Exasperating—by the time we were eighteen or so one was well aware that there was no competition. Game, set and match to Lavinia. She had that presence, and the smile . . .

*Though come to think of it, sitting here talking to this woman with her notebook and her recorder, it's actually match to me in the end, because I'm still alive and Lavinia isn't. The last word to me, as it were. And I can say what I like about her, except that I shan't. Getting tired of it. Tired of Lavinia. Just like her to go on being talked about after she's dead.*

Sorry? Well, the three of us, of course. My two brothers and me. Paul died last year and Stan's lost his marbles, poor old boy, doesn't know t'other from which. So you won't get anything out of them, I'm afraid.

*Though you would have done. They worshipped her, being male. The Lavinia effect.*

You know, I'm wondering if I've got all that much more to add that's any use to you. As I say, we weren't all that close.

By all means. Whenever. Just give me a ring.

*

Interview with Richard Beaver. Merrivale Road, Sevenoaks. June 28th 2014.

Lavinia. Lavinia. Just saying her name still has a certain potency. No, not the love of my life but an emotional landmark—put it that way. And she was pretty vibrant then, Lavinia—the sixties let her loose, she was all black leather, cropped hair, those sleeveless dresses. Her Sussex days, of course—trendy Ph.D. on family values in the early modern period, or words to that effect. She's still like that, in my mind's eye. I've never seen her since, except on the telly, of course. That series. I remember thinking: Christ, she must be fifty—trust Lavinia to give fifty a special flavor—kind of elegant mature laced with some sort of eternal *youngness* peeking through. I watched all of it. My wife was somewhat tight-lipped. Oh yes, she knew we'd been together, back then.

Almost inevitable, it seems now. There was she—pick of the postgrads. And there was I, youngest faculty member in this fashionable brand-new university, all of twenty-seven, cruising around those desperately state-of-the-art Basil Spence buildings, all of us academics handpicked to redraw the maps of learning or some such stuff, the students all state-of-the-moment, swanning about giving interviews to London journalists. Obviously, we'd notice each other, Lavinia and I. And noticing led to rather more, very quickly. Though we had to be not too conspicuous— faculty weren't to get involved with the students, even a postgrad with a three-year age difference. I remember being in a Chinese restaurant in Brighton with her, and in came the Dean of my School of Study with a party—it was all Schools of Study, not Departments, mind-blowing academic innovation. I got a bit panic-stricken, and said we should maybe sneak out before they saw us, but she wasn't having any of that. I can hear her now: "We're bloody well not going to, Richard. We're just having supper together—not fornicating."

You've got your work cut out, I'd say, writing about Lavinia. There'll be a minefield of comment. Have you seen Gerald Plant yet? I ran into him once at a conference—found myself at the same table. I said: "I used to know your wife—back in the Sussex days." He stopped eating, eyed me. Then—with bland smile: "Indeed? Some happy memories, no doubt." What was meant by that? Nothing at all—or: I know all about you, and you are of no interest to me.

Not yet? Ah. Have fun. He had a Chair at Oxford by then, Plant, and would have seen me as lesser fry altogether—you'll be aware of the vigorously hierarchical nature of the academic world. And Lavinia of course was everywhere—theoretically

rooted at her London college—Temple—but all over the air-
waves, open the Sunday papers and there she was. Wonderfully
adroit choice—that field of study. She owned all commentary on
family or children. Ironic, really, when . . . My wife was always
pointing that out, rather nastily. We had three, which may in
part account for my somewhat low publication record.

Oh Lord, look . . . I've got to pick a daughter up at the station,
I'd almost forgotten. Could we call it a day?

Yes. Yes, fine. Anytime.

*

Interview with Carol Pickering. University Women's Club. July
14th 2014.

Oh, she was such fun, Lavinia. We had a great time—sharing a
flat in Brighton. I was doing an MA, just, and of course my academic ambitions rather fizzled out, whereas she . . . And she
never seemed to be working, though she must have been, she got
the Ph.D., but she was always up for anything—the parties, the
jaunts to London for a raid on Biba. She was sixties to the hilt,
Lavinia. Me, too—goodness, you're bringing it all back. I've still
*got* a Biba dress somewhere—*Antiques Roadshow* stuff now, I suppose. But she was dead serious, too, underneath. She meant
business, where work and career were concerned. You knew she
was going to disappear over the horizon, sooner or later—which
of course she did. I never saw a lot of her, after Sussex—we kept
up, the occasional phone call, quick lunch in London, but I was
just a housebound mother, and then teacher in the local comp,
whereas she shot up the academic ladder and published book
after book and became, well, a big name.

Oh, no—she wasn't patronizing. Never, never. Lavinia wasn't
like that. She . . . she didn't need to be. People who patronize are
affirming their status, aren't they? And it would never have

occurred to Lavinia to do that. She couldn't be bothered, she had better things to do.

Confident? Well, yes, I suppose so, but never in an annoying way. It was a sort of private confidence. That French expression—*bien dans sa peau*. She was comfortable with herself, so you were comfortable with her. At least I was. I know not everybody . . . I suppose you're talking to various people . . . Look, take it from me, Lavinia was basically *all right*, whatever anyone says. Of course she must have trodden on a few toes, with a career like that, but she was fantastically interesting, and good to be with. And thoughtful in her way—sort of busy, rushed way, even back in Sussex. She held my hand when I had boyfriend trouble. Not something that came her way, much—men fell for her right and left. She was with Richard Beaver—oh, you've spoken to him. She shed him as soon as she'd left Sussex, I suppose you could say a bit hastily but that was Lavinia's style—if something wasn't working, didn't suit anymore, then move on. Jobs, places to live, men . . . I mean, that's so unlike my life that I've always admired it.

And I remember when . . . well, I lost a baby once, stillborn, and Lavinia came to see me right away, though I know she was frantically busy. Came to see me in Twickenham, where we were living then, John working in the City—made me come out for lunch, was funny and sympathetic both at once. Of course I had the other two but she didn't point that out or say, look, just get pregnant again fast. Though that's what I did . . . She was somehow so right for that situation. Made me laugh instead of cry.

Fond of children? I've no idea, really. She never saw anything of mine. Maybe not, since she never had any.

I last saw her . . . Goodness, now you're asking . . . I can't quite think. Not for—well, not for ages, I realize. We met for lunch in London. I'd dropped her a line to say I'd thought the TV series was terrific, and she suggested lunch so I came down specially, we were in Manchester by then.

Nineteen eighty-seven? That long ago . . . Well, if you say so. Yes, I suppose we had rather lost touch. I just slot into a bit of her life, don't I. I imagine that's why you wanted to talk to me. Witness to the 1960s.

*

Interview with Professor Gerald Plant. Merton College, Oxford. August 15th 2014.

We were married in the Registry Office in Oxford. In . . . 1970. 1972, was it? I stand corrected. You've marshaled the basic facts, evidently. Essential groundwork—I always used to tell students that. Oxford Registry Office—witnesses were an old friend of mine and a young colleague of hers—Mary . . . Mary something.

Mary Whittaker. Don't much remember her.

What did Lavinia wear? *Wear?* Well, a dress of some kind, I suppose. I'm sure she looked delightful—Lavinia always did.

No, no honeymoon. As such. Too busy, both of us. A week in Paris some while later—work-based to an extent, Lavinia wanted the Bibliothèque Nationale for research she was doing on nineteenth-century French infanticide rates, and my particular field as you will know is the Revolution, so I had business there too. But we found time for amusement as well. A trip to Chartres, I remember—Lavinia had never seen the cathedral. Lavinia was keen on experience: "I've never this . . . I've never that . . ." I hear her saying things like that still. So if you like you can say we had our honeymoon in Chartres cathedral. Or in the Bois de Boulogne—we went there one evening, as well. Either would fit the somewhat conjectural nature of biography. I'm not condemning your métier, not by any means, valuable stuff in some hands, in some respects, but I'm sure you'll agree that there is always an element of—shall we say—conflicting evidence. Uncertainty.

I beg your pardon?

Oh—history. Indeed, indeed. You have a point. The equivalent problem. The essential difference being the general context, the wider sweep. Though I suppose you will be trying to place Lavinia within some kind of context—her associates. Myself in particular, I suppose—twenty-five years of marriage, or thereabouts.

I'm sorry? My hearing is a touch imperfect. Thirty, was it? You realize of course that I was somewhat older than Lavinia. Ironic that I should have outlived her.

Yes, I heard you. I was considering. I prefer on the whole not to expand on the last ten—fifteen—years. No, we weren't together so much. Lavinia had a lot of commitments, I have a major work still in progress and needed to stay put, on the whole. She was in London, I was here.

Of course we were in contact. Just not together all the time.

Fifteen years? Thereabouts. You are, if I may say so, pursuing this to no great effect. It was merely a matter of convenience.

Her work. Well, of course I respected her work. Admired, in some areas. She pioneered much of what has been done with regard to the study of childhood and the treatment of children. Early on in her career. Valuable work. Mind, later, I suppose one has to say an element of populism rather prevailed.

No, I am not dismissive of television. A powerful medium, as one is grimly aware.

I don't think that history has a place on television? I haven't said that, nor would I. Lavinia was very eloquent in programs with a wide appeal, I don't doubt. Merely, I have never felt tempted in that direction myself. You must find others to assess her contribution to that area of historical studies—if that is an appropriate term.

No, I am not acquainted with Simon Schama.

Yes, she was indeed somewhat charismatic, I believe, among younger colleagues. I didn't come across them myself. Belinda Hemingford? That name does ring a bell, vaguely. In Lavinia's York days, you say? Well, I was then of course at East Anglia— my first professorial appointment, as I'm sure you know. We had the Norwich house, to which she returned every weekend, and held, I have to say, something of a salon—people invited all the time. Very popular with my colleagues—Lavinia's Saturday suppers. I suppose I had not been previously known for creative hospitality.

Creative? Well, she invited all sorts of people. I discovered aspects of the university quite unfamiliar to me. Sociologists. Media Studies. I was not always impressed.

Of course she did the cooking. Academic salaries do not run to employing caterers.

No, I am not able to cook.

What did she serve? Good heavens, I've no idea—so long ago. I may not have much noticed at the time. My task was to pour the drinks.

Beer. Modestly priced wine. Look, if I may say so, we are straying rather far from the essentials of Lavinia's life.

I shall have to reflect a moment on this . . . Let me see. If I am to describe her, Lavinia was . . . she was . . . Competent. Energetic. Purposeful. Well liked. Yes, people liked Lavinia.

I suppose so. *I* found her attractive. Others too, I dare say. Intellectually? It is hard to quantify an intellect. Lavinia was a good scholar—the early work is testimony to that. Possibly not . . . remarkable. Academia abounds in entirely competent scholarship. That occasional flare of genius . . . Lavinia did not perhaps have that. But a sound mind—definitely.

I would prefer not to discuss my own work.

Yes, we had shared interests. We both liked to walk. Offa's

Dyke, once. Wenlock Edge. Though these were rare excursions—neither of us able to take much time off. Travel, too—but, again, little opportunity. I do not much care for the theater—Lavinia did. Equally, I seldom watched television. Lavinia had what I suppose one must now see as a certain professional curiosity. I am rather less socially active than she was. Hmmn . . . I seem to be finding more points of departure than otherwise, but I think you can take it that we were a reasonably companionate married couple. And that is as far as I propose to go in consideration of my marriage, I am afraid. I hope you will understand.

A further occasion? If you wish.

*

Interview with Belinda Hemingford. University Women's Club. September 3rd 2014.

Goodness, it's hard to know where to *begin* with Lavinia. I mean, there's public Lavinia and private Lavinia, and for me she was both, really. We were in the same department at York—you know that—but she was older and established, and I was just an assistant lecturer, but she absolutely took me under her wing. She was like that with younger colleagues. If she approved of you. If she didn't . . . Well, she could be quite dismissive, Lavinia. Not everyone . . . But academia is red in tooth and claw, here and there—plenty of enmities.

Begin with public? OK. Terrific speaker—students flocked to her lectures. Great teacher. Active in university politics—furiously opposed to universities being taken over by the administrators—run by bureaucrats instead of academics, she used to say. It was the time when that was happening. And she was beginning to be noticed outside, around then, taken up by the BBC, you'd hear her on the radio quite a lot. Her big book came out then—*Love and Labor: The History of Childhood*. She sat on some major committee—Royal Commission on something. There was a profile of her in a Sunday newspaper—I've still got it somewhere, full-page photo, and there she was—very glam with that shoulder-length ash-blond hair, wearing black pencil skirt, red blouse, knee-high boots. That was how I felt about her, you realize, stashing away a newspaper clipping. But not everyone . . . There were people who didn't care for a tall poppy. Resented her. And of course she was up and off when she got the London professorship. They're probably more comfortable with tall poppies in London.

Private? Oh, well, *private*. And she was quite private, come to think of it. Even if you knew her pretty well—thought you did. Not the confessional type. I was with her a fair amount—she took me off on a working holiday once to France—"Come on—a week reading and writing by day, fine dining by night." Goodness, I was so thrilled. But she'd never talk about herself. Her views on what was going on in the world, gossip about colleagues, academic shop—plenty of all that. Funny, she could be. Sharp—not malicious, just occasionally barbed. People who'd got up her nose. So you see I realize I can say what she was *like*— a sort of climate of mind—clever and astute and kind—yes, kind—but critical and quite judgmental and ambitious, yes, but the kind of ambition that's about the thing being done, not the person doing it. So I can tell you the mind-set, as it were, but I really don't know what went on with her. What she felt. What— who—she cared about.

Her marriage. Oh, you've spoken to Gerald Plant. I see. I wonder how much speak there was . . . Casaubon personified, I always thought. Why on earth Lavinia . . . But a marriage is impenetrable, isn't it? I mean, Lavinia was thirty or so when they married, there'd been some relationship earlier that she ended, maybe she just needed a tether of some kind. Companionship. But how much of that she got from Gerald Plant . . .

Oh yes, he's highly regarded, as a historian. The last word on the French Revolution. One of the last words. Has his followers. Areas of patronage. I'm not in them. He's probably barely aware of me.

Children. Presumably they didn't want any. I can't see Lavinia as a mother.

Friends. Well, I suppose I can consider myself one. Though I didn't see *all* that much of her after York. She was so busy—so hither and thither. But we kept up. I'd always go to her for advice, for an opinion. She would read my stuff. Oh, she had various friends, Lavinia. I didn't know all of them, by any means. Men and women. She was good at men friends, without any sort of sexual element—at least so one assumes. There was that guy Steve Addison she worked with on the television series . . . But no, I don't think . . . No, I really don't. I don't think Lavinia had time for—well, for affairs, that sort of thing. Goodness, how have I got on to this? We're talking about *friends*. Yes, Lavinia had friends.

Sure—I'd be happy to talk to you again. I dare say there's all sorts of things I've forgotten for the moment. Yes, just e-mail me.

\*

Interview with Simon Barker. Highgate. September 20th 2014.

Lavinia Talbot. No, I don't find her an eccentric choice—just that she seems so recently with us, and now pinned out as biographical matter. Poor Lavinia, one feels, in a way—defenseless. I don't mean that as a criticism of your trade, but I think you'll see what I mean. I wonder what she would have felt about it.

Yes—colleague. Rather than friend, I have to say. And that—colleague—only in that we worked in the same institution. I'm not quite sure why you feel I'm the man to come to for the lowdown on Lavinia?

More detached view . . . Ah, I see. You've been the rounds of family and cronies. Well, detached is correct. Different department— I was Politics, as you know. But Lavinia was a big wheel in the college, you couldn't but be aware of her. Forceful committee woman. Persuasive, perhaps I should say. Good at getting what she wanted. Plenty of operative charm.

Did I like her? I suppose not. But you couldn't help being interested. The television work had made her something of a public figure. A celeb, as my daughter says. Academic celebs aren't so thick on the ground. And then she went even more public— chair of Enquiries and Royal Commissions and stuff, chair of the British Museum Trustees, all that. And her looks . . . that blond bob, her animated manner. She was striking to the end. I remember her on *Newsnight* not so long ago, it seems, banging the drum about attitudes toward childhood. And then, suddenly— obituaries. Cancer, was it? Ah.

Why was I less than keen on her? We had a few run-ins over college matters, but that wouldn't necessarily . . . more, she just felt to me somehow outside my remit. Mutual, I have to say— she didn't particularly notice me unless she had to. She had her acolytes, Lavinia, and I wasn't one.

She manipulated people. Fattened up her department with special posts for this and that—new Readership, a second Chair. All by sweet-talking in the right places. Those of us less talented in that direction felt upstaged. And then of course . . . outreach. The mistress of outreach, Lavinia. The BBC would have been lost without her—she reinvented the historical documentary. More or less banished dressed-up actors posturing around. Which meant more of *her*, of course—I dare say that was the idea. Though she presented well—that one has to admit.

Was it good history? Well, I'm hardly one to say—not my field at all. Can't say I watched all of it, anyway. My wife used to be rather glued, I remember.

Yes, there was a fair amount of sniping within the profession. Populist stuff, that sort of comment. I have some sympathy. And Lavinia was plugging her own particular interpretation, and those who disagreed couldn't respond, not having program makers at the BBC in their pocket. And rather more than that, as rumor had it.

No, nothing. Forget I said that.

Of course she was ambitious. You don't get where she did without plenty of maneuver. Single-minded, discard any impediments. No children, you note. And I doubt if Gerald Plant was allowed to be much of a hindrance. You've talked to him? Ah, you have. That is a diplomatic reply, I take it.

The books. Haven't read most of them. *Love and Labor* got a lot of attention—that's what really put her on the map, I suppose, when it came out. I did look at that, when she came to Temple. It was considered such a coup, getting her. Thought I'd better see what had been got. The book's quite a compelling read, I'll grant you that. Contentious, I gather, in parts. Arguing against earlier owners of childhood studies—Lawrence Stone, is it? People like that. New interpretation of attitudes toward childhood and the treatment of children. Well, people tend to be interested in that, not just academia, and she had a knack of accessible writing. I believe it made her a fair bit of money.

Really? No wonder she could dress the way she did. And that house in Primrose Hill.

Yes, once or twice. She gave parties. Even those on the outer rim of her radar got invited occasionally—such as me. No, I don't remember Plant being present. He had his Oxford Chair by then. Probably considered a London college outer suburbia.

Oh, there'd be all sorts there. Lavinia had a wide acquaintance. Academics, journalists, BBC people. Recognizable faces. My wife thought it a great lark—too easily impressed. I remember standing observing, with mild amusement. Ah, there's Bernard

Levin. And A. J. P. Taylor. And Huw Wheldon. She had an interesting address book, Lavinia. But most of the people then in it
are no longer with us, so you're reduced to the likes of me. Not
at all. Quite prepared to help if that's what I'm doing. Though
I'm beginning to feel anything more I have to say will be scrap-
ing the barrel. Some way on with the project, are you?

Loose ends . . . Indeed, if you think I can tie up any of those do
get in touch.

*What you do not know, of course, and never will, is that I found Lavinia*
*desperately attractive. That—all right—I lusted after her. That if in the*
*same room I had to steel myself not to keep looking at her. Just once, way*
*back, in her early days at Temple, I let myself indicate this, couldn't help it.*
*Made a pass, of a kind. And got the brush-off. Definitive. So definitive it*
*was as though the moment never was. Not the slightest indication from*
*her, ever, that it had happened. Steve Addison. Oh no, it wasn't just*
*rumor. So Steve Addison was in some other league, was he?*

*

Interview with Steve Addison. Muswell Hill. October 10th 2014.

Yes, of course, quite happy to talk about her. You get to know
someone pretty well when you work with them, and Lavinia
was fantastic as a colleague in that way. She became a real pro—
you forgot entirely that television wasn't her first calling. And we
learned from her—she gave us ideas, she innovated.

Well . . . the whole idea of the series was hers, of course.
Floated it in the right quarters. But then she soon persuaded us
to drop the enactments that were so often done—said: "I can *tell*
it, with the right background support. We don't need Italia Conti
kids playing Victorian factory workers." Absolutely—it worked.
Her elegant presentation, and all the images we had the research-
ers find, and the occasional film sequences, the readings . . .
Hugely emotive.

You have seen it. Good. So glad you agree. Yes, I always feel it was a seminal piece of filmmaking. We set a trend, I think. And Lavinia had a big hand in it. Without her suggestions it would have been done in a much more conventional way. In fact, it was because of her suggestions that the Beeb agreed to make it an eight-parter instead of the four originally planned. Exceptional—a prime-time history documentary of that length. *The Child in History*—my title, I may say. She always felt it too sweeping, because we weren't covering all history, she pointed out, just from the Middle Ages on—but I wanted something memorable. And it has been—memorable. The use of contemporary evidence—diaries, letters. Lavinia standing by that coal tip reading out the account of nineteenth-century child miners. The images we found, using them with Lavinia's voice-over. No dressed-up Italia Conti kids . . . Just sober, powerfully effective images, and language. Everything from eighteenth-century child hangings to the more endurable side—Little Lord Fauntleroy, literary presentations of childhood. Lavinia was immersed—she'd come to every meeting with a new burst of ideas— "Listen, I'm thinking that we could use *Silas Marner*. Children's play rhymes . . . Hogarth . . ."

She was . . . It was more than a work project for her—she was emotional about it. She was identifying, you felt, in some way. Sometimes she'd make us do a take again: "I was too—too committed. Again, please, more detached this time." But she wasn't detached—the whole thing was straight from . . . straight from the heart as well as the head. That's what made it so effective. Goodness—what a time that was, making it all.

Yes. Yes, I used to see something of her afterward.

Yes, I suppose you could say she had become a friend.

Look here—you *know*, don't you; I can see it in your expression. I wonder who told you.

Five or six years, we were lovers. After the filming. It began then, and went on. And never quite ended. We weren't lovers anymore but we'd talk, we'd have lunch now and again. Right up till . . . oh, six months or so before she died. And she never told me she was ill. Supper somewhere, all her news—but not that.

She was six years older than me. And after we broke up—well, stopped being lovers, we never *broke up*—I got together with Denise, who I'm still with. Not that you really need to know that—you're not interested in me, except as ancillary to Lavinia. And . . . I'm thinking that I'm *not* going to say all this is off the record, for your purposes. My relationship with Lavinia. Why should I? Denise knows. As for Gerald Plant—I don't really care. Maybe he knew anyway.

He didn't mention me? Well, he wouldn't, would he? Tight-arsed so-and-so, I thought, the only time I met him.

I never felt she was older. She had that extraordinary verve, energy, sense of fun. When you were with her, life went up a notch or two—brighter, sharper. Not that I was ever with her enough—snatched nights, a rare weekend, a week once in Italy. Not furtiveness on her part—more, her schedule. Though we *were* fairly furtive. She didn't want us to be common knowledge—though clearly . . . well, *you've* picked up on us somehow, all this time after. As for Plant . . . it was a pretty detached marriage by then, I doubt if they were often under the same roof. She never talked about him—referred to him occasionally in passing. I never had any idea what she felt about him. No guilt, I imagine: "I'm a married woman, I shouldn't be in bed with Steve Addison." I was a free spirit, myself—I'd had a relationship for quite a while which had ended before Lavinia came into my life.

Enriched my life. *Was* my life, I suppose, for that time. I adored her. And that's *not* for the record. There's a limit to Denise's tolerance.

Yes, you can ask that. Somehow . . . oh, I don't know—we didn't exactly drift apart, it was more there was less to the phys-ical side of things, it was warmth rather than passion, we were just seeing each other less often. And eventually not so much at all. But always a closeness, when we did meet. There was that feeling of shared time—shared history. And, dammit, I'm proud of that. Proud to have shared time with Lavinia Talbot. I think she was someone rather notable—and obviously you must too, or you wouldn't be doing what you are.

Notable how? Well, her work—and I count *The Child in History* as part of that—not just the books, her teaching, the whole academic shoot. All that public service, chairing this and that. I don't know so much about all that, though of course I read *Love and Labor*, we drew on it a lot for the series. A whole expression of mind, you could say—a productive and original mind. Notable for that. But there was herself too—the personality—and that's what is inaccessible for you, isn't it? Frustrating, it must be. You can look at photos, and read her, and hear what people say, but in the end you can't reach her. I'm realizing how odd it is—she is in my head, Lavinia, I see her and hear her—what we call memory—but I can't pass that on to you. I sit here, owning, as it were, all sorts of images, incarnations of Lavinia, and I can't share them, even if I wanted to, which in fact I don't.

Sorry, that sounds offensive. Don't mean to be. This is getting to me a bit, I'm finding.

Sure, sure. Another time. And I promise there won't be a further spiel like that.

*Actually, I'm not sure how much more there will be. I've said enough. Too forthcoming. She sits there, with that interested, inquiring expression— persuasive sort of woman—and you find yourself getting all confidential. Except of course that it isn't confidential—it's for a fucking book, Lavinia laid out for all and sundry.*

*But she's not, like I said. She's in the head. And you can't get at that, my friend, however interested and inquiring. There are shards of Lavinia—memory shards—that I own forever.*

*Lavinia in a bistro in France, that weekend we managed, laughing her head off at me trying to eviscerate a lobster.*

*Lavinia on the balcony of my flat, reading the paper, the sun on her hair.*

*Lavinia in bed. Oh, I never felt I was making love to a productive and original mind. I was making love to Lavinia, and minds didn't enter into it.*

*I'm keeping all that. Mine, and mine only. All that—and how Lavinia was. The private part of Lavinia. That part I felt I never reached. Some sort of basic hunger she had. Some sense of loss—I don't know . . . I wasn't going to talk to Ms. Biographer about that. Oh, no.*

*Now it's really getting to me, not like I made out just now, to get shot of the interview.*

*I can see her, feel her.*

*Shit. Come back, Lavinia.*

*

Phone conversation with Richard Beaver. October 21st 2014.

Richard Beaver here—you asked for a further word about Lavinia. This a good moment? Right—what did you want to know?

Ah. Did I not go into that—the end of our relationship?

Well, there's not much to go into really. She was leaving Sussex; I was staying. So if it was to continue there'd have been a problem of logistics. Sort of by mutual agreement, really, I remember—both feeling it had perhaps run its course anyway.

Not at all. No bother. Glad to have been able to help. I'll look forward to the book.

*Not particularly, in fact. Knowing at least one glaring inadequacy. Knowing what you'll never know, because only Lavinia and I ever did, and she would have told no one.*

*Abortion is an ugly word. Odd that I feel that, given that I insisted. We can't have a child. We may not even be going to stay together—did I say that? And she said: we might—we haven't tried. She was desperate—oddly desperate. Wanted it. And I said: look, you're young, there'll be other times. Not now, not this one. Which made perfect sense, of course. She didn't seem able to see that. So the deed was done, and that was that, between us. She went.*

*

Phone conversation with Professor Gerald Plant. November 4th 2014.

Plant here. Yes? Yes, I remember. Well, not entirely convenient but if it's just some small points I'd prefer to deal with them now rather than at some other time.

The house in Primrose Hill was her property, yes.

Computer? I remember her taking to the new technology with enthusiasm.

When and how did we first meet? She attended a symposium I had arranged. I was interested in her contribution, and invited her to join me for a meal afterward.

Yes. A mutual attraction, I suppose you could say.

Yes. We were married within a few months.

Yes, we had decided to get married quite quickly. And, as I have said before, I prefer not to discuss my marriage. I feel that I have no more to add that would be useful so if you have no further queries I would be grateful if we could conclude. Thank you. Good-bye.

*Nothing to add, and no need to go into detail for this young woman. Detail pertinent only to Lavinia and myself. The fact that she miscarried the baby was of great distress to her, though rather less so to me—I had not been all that keen on the idea of a family. Though quite prepared for an early marriage when it became apparent that Lavinia was pregnant. Which never happened again. I believe that was a matter of regret, for her. A private matter, inappropriate to this woman's book.*

*

Julia Pemberton's timely biography of Lavinia Talbot is an incisive account of the life of a remarkable woman, remembered for her trenchant and absorbing academic studies on the treatment of children over time, and perhaps especially for her groundbreaking television series *The Child in History*. Distinguished equally for her work in public service, Lavinia Talbot was a vibrant and compelling personality, and Julia Pemberton has made an exhaustive exploration of her life and work. The result is a fascinating and truthful portrait.

Publication date November 14th 2015. All inquiries to Lizzy James at Cavendish Books.

Julia Pemberton is available for interview.

# The Weekend

The Dennisons were on their way to spend the weekend with the Sanderbys. At the Sanderbys' new Cotswold second home. Philip and Vanessa Dennison; Nick and Jill Sanderby. And Martha Dennison, who was eight, and sat in the back of the car, silent.

"All right, darling?" said Vanessa. An eight-year-old who has been silent for a considerable time is suspect. Car sick?

"I'm OK."

"Sure?"

Martha was understood to say, quietly, that she didn't really want to go and spend the weekend at the Sanderbys' new house.

Vanessa, no longer concerned, spoke of country walks and a little bedroom of her own.

"There'll be no one to play with. You said they haven't got any children."

Vanessa mentioned a possible television in this customized room. And Martha's new coloring things. She herself was not on a mission of potential pleasure but a sortie into alien territory. Alien, and probably challenging.

An Aga, she thought. Bet you an Aga. And a wet room. Wood-burning stove and en suites to every guest room and dresser with interesting old china and floodlights in the driveway.

Philip was an academic. Academics do not have second homes in the Cotswolds, with or without Aga, wet room, en suites. Philip and Nick had been at college together, since when their paths had diverged.

Vanessa had Googled Nick. Google spoke of him as "millionaire City lawyer." Google is dispassionate, so this could not be read as respectful nor condemnatory. Vanessa knew how she read it. Philip and Nick had met up at some alumni gathering recently, when this weekend proposal had been floated, and followed up with a florid card of invitation from Jill: ". . . so longing to see you, and now the house is all kitted out at last we can entertain *properly.*"

"She hardly knows us," Vanessa had said. "Display of circumstances, that's what this is. His megabucks pay packet and their country mansion."

Philip shook his head, vaguely. He and Nick had been quite good friends, back in that alternative world of youth. Academic highfliers, both of them; college aristocracy.

Vanessa continued: "Does she do anything, Jill?"

Philip said that Nick had talked of her agency. "It organizes parties, I think. Events of one kind and another."

"Oh, *gawd.*" Vanessa worked as a copy editor for a publishing group. She was able to feel dismissive: who needs party organizers? A rubbish occupation.

"Oh, well," she had said. "We may as well go. See how the other half lives."

And now, according to the sat nav, here they were. Driveway with scrunchy gravel, yes. Not mansion, exactly, but substantial honey-colored house swathed in wisteria.

A million plus, thought Vanessa. Of course. And there's the Range Rover.

Philip was a scholarly man who took no interest in house prices. He saw mauve flowers, a large red car, and Jurassic stone, wouldn't it be, round here? Yes, oolitic limestone. Paleontology was not his subject, but he tended to know things.

The front door opened. Here were Jill and Nick, enthusiastically greeting.

"And Martha! Hello, Martha! There's a darling little room for you—the Rose Room, we call it, because I went mad with rose-covered wallpaper." Jill seized bags. "Is this hers? Come on in."

No welcoming Labrador, thought Vanessa. That's an omission. Grandfather clock, yes. Open fireplace with stash of logs. Flower arrangement—but are those not *bought* flowers?

Allocation of rooms. Martha went to her window and looked out over a garden. Huge garden. With a separate sort of secret little garden at the end where a swing hung from the branch of a tree. The swing moved; it swung a bit, to and fro.

There was tea in the kitchen. The sort of kitchen anticipated; I have to stop looking and bristling, thought Vanessa. She talked brightly of the drive down here: "Really not bad traffic at all." Nick said that in the Range Rover they reckoned to get back to town in two hours max. Philip talked about oolitic limestone and wondered if there had been a quarry nearby. Jill and Nick looked blank. Jill said they were lucky, there was a really good little deli in Chipping Campden. "You'll sample it tonight."

Martha ate chocolate cake, in silence.

Later, there was a tour of the garden.

"Except that it isn't, yet," said Jill, waving at expanses of shabby lawns, overgrown bushes, grass-infested paving. "All in hand, though. There's an excellent local firm, and they've done a lovely plan—complete overhaul. Starting work next month—it's going to be rather something." The party wandered through the damp grass, Vanessa concerned for her thin shoes, Jill talking about a laburnum walk, a sunken rose garden.

"And this funny little space at the end," she continued. "I'm not quite sure what they've got in mind for that." She led the way through a high yew hedge. A couple of huge old apple trees. Sprawling bushes. Even longer and damper grass.

Martha was looking at the swing.

"I wonder if it's safe," said Jill. "I'm not too sure about that, darling."

Philip tugged at the ropes; the sturdy branch of the apple tree hardly moved. He bounced the seat up and down. "Seems all right. D'you want a go, Martha?"

Martha was very still, looking at it. She shook her head.

"Fruit area down here," said Jill. "Yes, that's what they're thinking of. Get it all dug over and have raspberries and all that sort of thing. Come along now—it's getting on for drinks time." She murmured to Vanessa and Philip that she had rather imagined that Martha did not stay up for grown-up dinner. Vanessa said that was indeed so. Just a bit of early supper, if that's not a bother.

A weekend visit like this revolves round eating, thought Philip. Dinner tonight, breakfast, lunch . . . He was already realizing that there was really no longer much to talk to Nick about; young Nick seemed some other being. He found Jill a bit exhausting.

They returned to the house. "The chaps can have a natter in Nick's study," said Jill. "And we'll sort out some supper for Martha, shall we?"

Nick's study had an immense fitted bookcase with nothing much in it except for some law books. Large desk; computer, printer, iPad. Couple of leather armchairs.

They sat. Nick talked about the establishment of a branch in Hong Kong, for their firm: "I dare say I shall find I need to go and check up on it once or twice a year. I love Hong Kong." He spoke of a complex recent case. At length.

Philip thought about parliamentary enclosure in the eighteenth century, his current preoccupation. He was good at mental retreat, practiced it in prolonged departmental meetings, and occasionally at home, when Vanessa was on a roll about something.

He became aware of silence. "Extraordinary," he said. "Fascinating."

Nick smiled complacently. "And we won, of course. Anyway . . ." He seemed, now, to be flailing a bit. "How's life in academia? Working on something?"

Philip thought of talking about parliamentary enclosure, and decided against it. A mere handful of people were likely to be interested in his eventual article, in any case, and Nick would not be among them. He slid sideways into an account of problems with increasing student numbers, and the university's new building program. He wondered how Vanessa was getting on.

In the kitchen, Vanessa and Martha were watching Jill muster an omelet and some salad. "And then there's ice cream in the freezer. Can she?"—to Vanessa.

Vanessa said that she could. She hated this kitchen, from its rich green Aga (of course) through the row of copper pans slung from one wall, and the butcher block, and the dresser with pretty Victorian china (of course) and the shelf of Le Creuset casseroles in every size and shape. She hated it because she wanted it.

Martha said, "Our kitchen isn't like this."

Jill laughed. "Well, this is a *country* kitchen."

Vanessa said that Martha would be ready for bed as soon as she'd had her supper. "Won't you, darling?"

Presently the two of them climbed the stairs to the Rose Room and its attendant bathroom. Martha had a bath. Vanessa said, "I'm afraid it's a bit dull for you here. Never mind—home tomorrow evening."

"I like the garden," said Martha.

"I've got to get ready for dinner now. Our room is just along the passage, if you want anything in the night."

Martha said she thought she would be all right.

Drinks outside, before dinner.

"Do you think a hot tub on the terrace would be completely naff?" said Jill. "I would rather love one."

Philip wondered what she was talking about. Vanessa had no opinion. She was considering whether to drink as much as possible and become mercifully oblivious, or whether to hold back in case drink prompted some unwise remark. By the time they went in for dinner she was somewhere in between these two positions.

Philip was still interested in this matter of local stone. He tended to wrestle with a subject. "A lot of the Oxford buildings came out of these quarries, I believe. And there's some special slate—Stonesfield, I think. Yes, Stonesfield. Does this house have a Stonesfield slate roof?"

"Oh, I imagine so," said Jill. It sounded as though that sort of roof was the thing to have. "Of course, we were incredibly lucky to get the house. They tend to get snapped up. But we did the snapping—the previous owners were in a hurry to sell—they'd had a child die and just wanted to get away and live somewhere else. Tragic, of course, but a bit of luck for us. We jumped in with an offer rather over the asking price, and here we are." She beamed across the table, over the gravad lax starter.

Definitely more wine, thought Vanessa. It's the only way. She reached for her glass, emptied it.

Jugged hare, there was next. "Of course, I didn't jug it myself," laughed Jill. "The local deli does these really good frozen meals. A godsend, when we arrive from town after a hectic week."

Please don't let's hear about your hectic week, prayed Vanessa. But they did: some event at the O2, and a wedding at the top of the Shard. Philip retreated to parliamentary enclosure; Vanessa toyed rather obviously with her empty glass. Nick opened another bottle.

The jugged hare gave way to a fruit salad. Vanessa excused herself: "I must just pop up and see Martha's all right."

She found Martha asleep. She had fallen asleep easily. The room seemed quite companionable, as though somehow she was not alone.

Vanessa returned to the party, finding that she had to take extra care on the stairs. No more wine, she thought. It's probably done the trick now anyway. She allowed the conversation to lap around her rather than join in and risk being either irrelevant or provocative. She was nicely sleepy, in any case.

Eventually, the evening ended. Upstairs, in their room, Vanessa said, "I'm completely sloshed. It was the only thing to do, wasn't it? Are you?"

Philip yawned. "Mildly so. Is it that bad here?"

"Yes," said Vanessa.

"One feels rather out of place, certainly. Sorry to have let you in for it."

"Never mind." Vanessa could afford to be generous, in an alcoholic haze. "I dare say he was perfectly all right when he was young. You couldn't know how he would develop. Or who he would marry."

Philip sighed. "We don't seem to be on the same wavelength. No doubt he's thinking the same."

"Let him. All we have to do is get through tomorrow. We can leave smartly at five or so—plead Sunday evening traffic."

Next morning, Vanessa found that the comfort of alcohol had soured into a hangover. She dragged herself down for breakfast and drank a lot of coffee. Jill was unrelentingly bright, enthusing about the lovely sunny day, the fresh croissants from the village shop, the prospect of lunch out at a local eaterie. "More gastro than pub, if you see what I mean. Amazing chef." The morning could be spent ". . . any way you like. Nick got the Sunday papers along with the croissants. Or a walk, if anyone wants."

Martha spoke up, surprising her parents. "Can I go in the garden?"

"But of course." Jill beamed. "Do whatever you like there."

Philip said that he would quite like a walk. As he had feared, Nick declared that he would join him. Jill would stay here to keep Vanessa company.

The morning proceeded. Vanessa's planned retreat into the Sunday papers was sabotaged by Jill's constant interventions and tendency to read out loud some item she had come across: "Do listen to this . . ."

At one point Vanessa went to check up on Martha, wading again through the damp grass. She found her sitting on the swing, looking as though somehow interrupted. No, Martha said, she didn't want any juice. Or a biscuit. She was fine.

Vanessa returned to the terrace. Jill said, "What a good little thing she is, amusing herself on her own like that. I heard her *laughing* just now."

"She's had to learn to, as an only." Vanessa regretted this at once, expecting interested comment, or some revelation about Jill's own childlessness, but Jill merely embarked on an account of recent visitors, whose child had been an absolute pain.

The men returned. Time for the lunchtime excursion. Martha, summoned, asked if she could stay here.

"By yourself?" snapped Vanessa. "Of course not."

Martha began to say something. Fell silent. Remained so throughout the meal in the pub. Her parents were also subdued. Philip had heard about another case of Nick's, in unremitting detail, over several fields and through an otherwise delightful bluebell wood. Vanessa now knew that Jill had a resident housekeeper in London ("Spanish, brilliant, quite simply keeps the show on the road for us") and that her clothing needs were attended to by a personal shopper ("She sources everything and saves me all that traipsing around—I can give you her name").

Lunch ended. Vanessa felt gastronomically assaulted. Philip

had indigestion. Back at the house, there were more Sunday papers and desultory chat on the terrace. Martha vanished.

And, at last, the moment came when Vanessa could decently propose departure. She went upstairs to pack up their things, and came down in rather better spirits.

She put their bags in the hall and went out onto the terrace. "Martha! Martha! We're going now."

Jill was saying that they must come again sometime. "We're rather booked up for the rest of the summer, but it's lovely here in autumn." Nick was proposing lunch at his club, to Philip: ". . . must get together again at some point."

"*Martha!* Philip, could you go and round her up?"

Philip wandered off into the garden. Vanessa stood about, exchanging niceties. Philip returned, towing an apparently reluctant Martha. There were good-byes all round. The Dennisons piled into the car. The Sanderbys stood waving. Gravel crunched under the tires. "Good-bye, good-bye."

"Whew," said Vanessa.

"Sorry," said Philip.

"Never mind." Generosity could again be afforded. "Part of life's rich pattern." Vanessa turned to Martha. "All right? Sorry it wasn't much of a weekend for you."

"Oh, we had a really nice time."

Vanessa swung round. "We . . ."

"You told me they didn't have any children," said Martha. "So who was the girl in the garden?"

# License to Kill

"Coat," she said. "No, the red one, please."

The girl got the red one, stood there with it.

"Scarf, please. Gray scarf."

"Shopping list!" said the girl. Pouncing, triumphant.

"Put butter. I forgot. And J-cloths." She was eighty-six, and forgot much. The mind was porous; some things lodged, others did not.

The girl wrote. And drew a cat with whiskers, back view of. And a smiley face. She was eighteen. Might try that Aussie shampoo. Might go to Oxford Street with Lindy, at the weekend.

They went out of the front door. Cally said, "Shall I do the mortise lock, Pauline?"

"Yes—do it." The agency had asked if she would rather be Miss, and she'd said not. Hospitals don't now, either, one had noticed. Neither here nor there, as far as she was concerned, so long as they knew who you were.

Slow and careful on the steps, for her. Cally jumped the last three, stood at the bottom checking her phone, remembered she wasn't supposed to when working, shoved it in her pocket. She said, "Shall we get a coffee when we're in Marks?"

Pauline considered. Coffee, and one might need a loo before this shopping expedition is done. There's the bank, and Boots.

"Mmn. Maybe." You plot, daily. Face down circumstance. Measure out your life with . . . not coffee spoons—pills. Line them up with breakfast, lunch, supper. Never mind mermaids, and lilacs in bloom, and all that stuff. He hadn't a clue. In his twenties, wasn't he? It's pills, and have I phoned the surgery, and did I pay that gas bill, and have I got my debit card?

Have I?

She delved in her bag. Ah—there. Shall I eat a peach?

"Peaches," she told Cally. "Stick them on the list."

"You said they never got ripe, last time."

"I'll persist. Dare. Maybe we will have a coffee, too."

In the bank, Cally had to put the number into the cash dispenser for her. Not easy to see them, now.

Cally said, "That bank person's staring at me. Thinks I'm up to no good. Using your PIN."

"I'd better give him a smile. There. He's lost interest—I am not under coercion."

"Mind," said Cally. "If you were going to nick someone's card and march them to the bank, they'd hardly just go along with it and stand there watching."

"They might if they'd lost their marbles. What he was thinking, perhaps."

"Three twenties and two tens. I've put them in the purse. And the card. Here . . . Boots next?"

I can look at the shampoos while she's waiting for her prescription, she won't mind. That's the thing about this job—there's spare time, sort of. Easy, and spare time, and this Pauline's fine, not like her in Brunswick Gardens—do this, do that, and never a thank you. Ninety-five, that one is. How can a person be ninety-five years old?

They found a chair for Pauline, by the prescription counter.

"Yes—go and browse. I shall be here for some time, I can see."

And time is no longer of the essence. It is baggy stuff, disposable, no need to preserve, allocate. Actually, that's a legal term, isn't it? Of the essence. To do with contracts. In non-legal life you just mean the need to hurry.

I have hurried, she thought. I have been hurried. Now, I no longer hurry. Days are capacious, to be idled through. Butt ends of my days. Oh, for heaven's sake, enough of that stuff. Mental sediment—all that was once read. Extraordinary, the accretion of it all. What one has done, what one vaguely knows. The arbitrary archive.

The pills came. Whole bag of them. The ones to be taken before a meal, the ones after, the ones with. The pharmacist inspected the haul: "I think you're familiar with all these?"

"Tiresomely familiar."

The pharmacist was young, Asian, pretty. Delicate small hands folded the bag shut and passed it to Pauline. Nice smile.

"Thank you."

Science A levels. Degree also, I think. The world will always need pharmacists. Wise girl. In fact, will need them more and more, with the expanding horde of the likes of me. Dispense pills, or make them—that's the business to be in.

Cally had returned, with Boots bag.

"Satisfactory?" said Pauline.

"I'm trying a new shampoo." And black nail polish, but she wouldn't care for that.

Marks & Spencer was the serious challenge: Pauline's grocery requirements. They began to work along the aisles. A slow process. Pauline was a judicious shopper. She peered, considered.

Cally pushed the trolley. She drifted, in the head, eyed people, fished for her phone, remembered and put it back. She needed to text Lindy, and Mum—that would have to wait. Nice—that girl's jacket. Zara? Oh yuck, that kid with a runny nose. If I have children . . .

She thought briefly of these unimaginable children. Binned them. Too far away. Well, out there somewhere, but not of interest just now.

Saturday night? Nothing fixed up. Lindy? Or that Dan? They were in Vegetables. "Where do these beans come from?" said Pauline.

"Kenya."

"Ah. Large carbon footprint, then. Still, I want some."

Kenya. One had a spot of bother once in Mombasa. Had to use the whole bag of tricks. I'd know him now—the face. And the name. But I can't put a tag on that woman I met last week. "Mustard," she told Cally. "I forgot that."

"OK. We'll get there. You've still potatoes and salad things."

"Right. And use your phone while we're having coffee. That's fine by me."

"Oh," said Cally. "There's no need. I . . ."

"I noticed you wanting to, dear," said Pauline. "Tea break coming up."

Embarrassed, Cally focused on lettuce. Many forms of lettuce.

"Do you like the mixed baby leaves?"

"No, let's have those Little Gems. Absurd name. Small lettuces, they are."

"My dad grows them, I think. Gardening's his thing. I used to like helping him but I've gone off it. The worms and stuff. I'm more of an indoor person."

"So what's in mind for the long term? You don't want to be dancing attendance on old women indefinitely."

"Oh, no," said Cally. "I mean . . . well, I mean I really like it, of course, but . . ."

"But with all options open. Quite right."

When I was her age, thought Pauline, the options were confusing. They always are. Who'd be young? Everything wide open, which means that the not chosen is discarded. Junked. I have junked being policewoman, interior decorator, estate agent, High Court judge, Home Secretary.

"I'm wondering a bit about nursing," said Cally.

"Only a bit?"

"I'm not sure about blood. I've not been awfully good with that."

"I imagine you get inured to it," said Pauline. "But if in doubt, maybe look elsewhere."

"I like cooking. My mum thinks perhaps a catering course. City and Guilds there is. Hospitality and Catering."

"Nice idea. Distinct possibility. Now, where are the potatoes?"

"Over here. Is it baking you want?"

"Jersey Royals. Or are we in the wrong time of year?"

Yes. Spring, they are. And this is autumn. For a moment I was untethered. Adrift in time. Alarming. But now I am hitched again to a Tuesday in October, and in need of a rest. "We'll head for the coffee place," she said. "My knee is complaining. Grab a bag of small potatoes and find us somewhere to sit."

Cally organized a table, queued up for two coffees, rejoined Pauline.

"Good. We've earned this." Pauline took a sip of her coffee.

"Hot. Have to leave it a minute. You do your texting now— rest period."

Feeling a little exposed, Cally told her mother she was in Marks with the Albert Street lady, who was OK, nice in fact, and I'll let you know about Sunday this evening. She arranged Lindy for Saturday. She nudged Dan. She drank her coffee.

"Yes," said Pauline. "Why don't you investigate this catering idea. Might lead to all sorts of things. Oh, it's such a teaser—the road not taken. Do you know that poem? 'Two roads diverged in a wood, and I / I took the one less travcled by.' Hackneyed, rather, now, but he had a good point."

"I expect you were a teacher, Pauline, were you?" said Cally kindly.

Pauline finished her coffee. "No, dear. I was a spy." She collected her bag, her stick. "Well, we'd better get on, I suppose."

They got up. Cally followed Pauline. She saw her looking much as she had before. Really old. Those thick glasses. The stick. But looking also . . . different. She was talking about chicken now, Pauline. Something about how she roasts a chicken with tarragon and lemon.

Cally stared at the chicken carcasses. "License to kill?" she ventured.

"Well, yes. But it wasn't called that. There was a euphemism. Find me the small size, could you—I can never finish the medium ones."

"Were you . . ." said Cally. "Did you spy sort of on your own?"

"No, no. It's an organizational operation. Have you heard of MI5 and MI6?"

Cally said that she had.

"Well, then. And it's less James Bond than you'd think. Office work, to an extent." Pauline examined a proffered chicken. "That one will do nicely."

Office, and what one might call exit periods. Most of which are still there with absolute clarity. Not in chronological order, and richly peopled. Oh, people above all—a filing cabinet of faces. One was always good at filing faces, of course.

They had reached oil and dressings. "Which mustard?" asked Cally. "And we want olive oil."

Like onions, she thought. A person is. Layers. And you haven't a clue. You just look at the top. An old person's just an old person, you think. Anyone is. Her there in that awful pink skirt too short for her, my mum's age she is. And him with the dreadlocks.

She said, "Did you . . . spy . . . go spying . . . in lots of far-away places?"

"A good Italian oil, I like," said Pauline. "And a lemon-flavored one."

Chimborazo, Cotopaxi . . . In fact one never made it to either of those. Nor yet Popocatépetl. But Mogadishu . . . No, this lass doesn't need to know about that episode in Mogadishu. Or Kinshasa.

"I suppose I did. It tends to be a global procedure. But forget speedboats on blue Bermuda waters or car chases in Singapore.

More, waiting about in train stations and meeting up with people one would have preferred to avoid."

"I'd like to travel," said Cally.

"Said to broaden the mind. Though that depends rather on the condition of the mind in question. I have known some well-traveled minds that were nicely atrophied. Now—how's that list? Where should we be heading?"

"Marmalade. With J-cloths later. I've been to the Algarve," said Cally. "I tried to learn a bit of Portuguese. Please and thank you, at the least."

But Pauline didn't go on Thomson Holidays, she thought. I don't know what she did, or what that person she once was did, but it can't have been lying on the beach and looking for the right *taberna*. Not if licensed to kill. She stared at Pauline's back. Tweed-clad, somewhat bent, inscrutable.

Pauline stumped ahead, thinking again about faces. That gallery in the head. From a display of grapefruit, a particular mug-shot surged. Yes, yes, she said. I remember you. Without enthusiasm.

Training, of course. An essential technique. What you didn't know was that you would be stashing them away forever.

A known face among the avocados, too—not unwelcome, but irrelevant, now. Get away with you, she told him. I'm through with all that, and so are you, wherever you are.

"Actually, we're the wrong way," said Cally. "We want to be over there."

"Aim me at marmalade, then."

Time was, one was pretty good at direction. Which came in handy, on occasion. Saved the situation, indeed, once. Peculiarly nasty area of Marrakesh.

She came to a stop. "Thick-cut. Golden Shred. Lime, is that, for heaven's sake? Who needs all these? Where's plain Oxford? Right. What else?"

"I'll nip down there for the J-cloths," said Cally. "Then we're done."

When she returned, Pauline was considering her purchases.

"There's an awful lot here. Are we going to be able to manage it?"

"Oh, yes. With your trolley thing. It holds ever so much."

"Right. Let's get done with this, then."

Queues at every checkout. "Maybe here," said Pauline. They lined up. Pauline noted that the woman ahead lived alone, had a cat, a weakness for milk chocolate, liked a glass of wine, planned to clean her oven and polish some silver. It dies hard, she thought, the instinct to observe, identify. Tiresome, rather, nowadays. I don't need to know about this lady's home life.

"Bear in mind," she told Cally, "that whatever you do choose as occupation, in due course, will form the habits of a lifetime."

"You mean, Hospitality and Catering and I'll think canapés and cupcakes for ever?"

"It goes with the territory, I imagine. I am doomed to pry, and make informed guesses. But today I have made a bad choice. Wrong queue, we're in."

Two customers ahead of them, trouble had brewed. A man had loudly pointed out that his egg carton included one that was broken. ("Should have checked, shouldn't he?" said Cally.) A replacement had been sent for but now he was in dispute with the cashier over whether or not the chicken korma was included in the mix and match offer.

"It said so. I saw quite clear."

"You see, it means . . ."

"It's what was said. You telling me I can't read?"

The dispute smoldered. The queue grew restive. Pauline leaned against a display of fruit gums.

"Way back, in my training days," she said, "I went on that course where you learned how to strangle a person with the bare hands. I think I am about to exercise the skill for only the second time."

Cally looked at her. Blinked. Looked away. Looked back, and Pauline was checking her purse for her debit card: dumpy, gray hair, that coat slightly worn at the cuffs. She did say that. Yes, she did.

Some accommodation had been reached, ahead. The man gathered his bags and departed.

"Just as well," said Pauline. "He was quite a big chap. Ah— here's my card. Now, are we really going to get all this in?"

The shopping was paid for, stowed away. They emerged into the street. Pauline paused to hitch her bag over her shoulder. "There. Thank you, dear. Mission accomplished."

Not that one ever said that. Merely—returned to the office and set about filing the report. Now, I file for my own satisfaction, and today is a reasonable day, with my knee not too bad, and those autumn leaves are as though never seen before and look, just look, at the berries on that sorbus.

Cally did not see leaves or berries. She saw street, cars, people, all much the same as half an hour ago but somehow vaguely unreliable. She felt, oddly, older. A slightly different person, who knew more. Who knew to make adjustments. Maybe not Catering and Hospitality, she thought. I may not be a Catering and Hospitality person. I don't know who I am yet, do I? Who I may be.

# Mrs. Bennet

In deepest Devon, in 1947, Mrs. Bennet lived on. Not as such, you understand, fictional or otherwise, but in the person of a Mrs. Landon, Frances Landon, who was married to a man of deficient means, and had three daughters, now of marriageable age.

The Landons had moved from Berkshire to Devon when the youngest daughter, Imogen, left school at sixteen. Pamela—now twenty—and Clare, eighteen, had also left at that age. They all had a taste for country life. Ted Landon's best attempts at successful work had been rural-based. Berkshire was edging toward suburbia, and, crucially, was without the sort of real country gentry that it would be promising for the girls to meet. You needed deep country, the shires. They would have to move.

A nice house was found, eventually, on the edge of a village in Devon, foothills of Exmoor. Pretty little nineteenth-century house with outbuildings, good garden, paddock, and an extension that could do for Ted's study or office.

Ted Landon drank a bit. Well, more than a bit. He had had a quiet war, tucked away in the War Office in some menial position, and had perhaps picked up the habit then, whiling away solitary evenings when his wife and the girls were safely away from the bombs. He was supposed, now, in Devon, to be helping out a local land agent, but little helping got done. The land agent had picked up, early on, that Ted was not likely to be sparking on all cylinders after his lunchtime break in the Red Lion, and called on him less and less. Before the war, Ted had tried apple farming, and chickens, and cattle feed salesman, but none of these had seemed to be quite his métier.

He was fifteen years older than Frances. She had married him in a panic, when twenty-four, with no one else in sight and spinsterhood staring her in the face, she felt. Dread word, not yet at its last gasp, nowhere near, indeed, bouncing ominously back in the wake of the Great War. Men were at a premium; young, marriageable men were gold dust, sought after, fought over. The debutante dances of the early 1920s were red in tooth and claw, and Frances had not made a kill. She saw contemporaries succeed, and sail off into the sunset with a ring on their finger, or fail, and fade away to help Mummy in the garden, or do good works. In the circles in which Frances moved the Pankhursts had been referred to with shock and disapproval; a nice finishing school was all a girl needed—a course at a Constance Spry place. Which Frances had done; she could arrange flowers, bake a cake, whisk up a soufflé, cook sole meunière. She could smock a baby's dress, knit a sock, iron a shirt. Groomed for homemaking, she was. And then there were no men. Except for Ted Landon.

It had not been a bad marriage. Not too bad. The girls had been the great thing, arriving in quick succession, and Ted's inability to make a success of anything had become only gradually apparent. Apple farming was hard work; battery chickens brought in no money at all, by the time you'd paid the men and the overheads; cattle feed salesman was frankly demeaning.

What was in mind was unspoken, but they were all aware—Frances positively so, the girls nervously but dutifully. Ted perhaps not at all, comfortably inured with the *Sporting Times*, his pipe, and a brandy or two.

Once settled in the Devon house, everything nicely put to rights, Frances looked about her. She soon saw that they did things differently here. Suburbia was far away. Here, the lanes rang to the sound of horses' hooves; daily, girls on nicely groomed ponies clattered past their door, done up in jodhpurs and hacking jackets. Young men, too. Periodically, the hunt poured past; hounds with waving sterns, the red-coated hunts-men, the whole field—an acreage of horseflesh, jodhpurs, hunting coats, bowlers. Girls, men.

They attended the Boxing Day meet at Churleston Manor, and stood on the fringes while the field milled about, reaching down from horseback to take a glass of sherry and a mince pie, shouting greetings: "That the new mare, Jane? Super." "Good to see you out again, Oliver. Arm all mended, is it?" The four Landons looked and listened. Nothing was said, but everything was understood.

The girls were going to have to get into the hunting field.

"But, Mummy, we can't ride."

That could be addressed. The local riding school was run by a Polish cavalry officer (or so he said). Colonel Kowalski was a part of the Second World War diaspora, washed up in Devon after heaven knows what wartime adventures, and nicely filling the slot left by the death of the aging lady who had formerly been instructing the county's young. Colonel Kowalski had the indoor school refloored, the outdoor manège returfed and refenced, and acquired a stable of ponies and horses of requisite size and temperament. The establishment was seen as vastly more professional.

The girls bumped round and round the indoor school and the manège, shouted at by the Colonel. "Hup-hup-hup, Pamela. Clare—keep that pony's head up. Heels *down*, Imogen, *down*."

After months, and considerable expenditure, the Colonel declared that Pamela at least could be considered a reasonably competent rider. Most work had been done on Pam, for obvious reasons. This was to be a carefully paced venture: Pam first, then the others in due course.

But there was more to come, much more. If you ride, you need a horse.

This was where Mrs. Halliday came in. Marcia Halliday was

the neighbor beyond the Landons' paddock, inhabiting a small thatched cottage that seemed inappropriate for its owner, a woman of patrician gentility, whose icy upper-class speech could freeze a room. She rode, she hunted. No, she lived for riding and hunting—out with the South Devon twice a week, the East Devon now and then, not forgetting the Devon and Somerset Staghounds. Her two horses occupied the field adjoining the Landons' paddock. Frances had struck up an acquaintance— passing, it seemed, Marcia Halliday's forensic social scrutiny, and when she confided that the girls were learning to ride and, well, Pam would love to have her own pony, Marcia had taken an interest. This was her territory entirely; possibly she sensed the general purpose, and saw the point. There was no Mr. Halliday in sight, but presumably there had been one.

Marcia Halliday took the whole thing in hand. After a brisk sourcing operation she came up with Willow, a rather inaptly named gray cob, solidly built, fifteen hands, not much to look at, which was why he came relatively cheap, but sound in wind and limb. Marcia tried him out on a day with the South Devon, and said that for her he would be on the slow side but she thought he might do well for Pam: nice temperament, didn't shy or kick, not much good over fences but she had the impression Pam wasn't that keen on a jump anyway.

Pam was not. Jumps filled her with horror. Colonel Kowalski had forced her over the two-bar in the manège and then the three-bar, less than knee-high: "Lift up into it, Pam, lift up. He can feel you holding back, so he does." Pam clung to the horse's neck, heart thumping, stayed on, just about, came down on the other side. No, she was not keen on a jump.

Willow was installed in the paddock. One of the outbuildings became the harness room. Frances had had no idea a horse required so much equipment: the saddle, bridle, halter, blanket for winter. The brushes, the sponges, the buckets, the saddle soap. The bales of straw for the other outbuilding, converted to a stable. The oats. The expense.

And then there was Pam herself. Smarter jodhpurs than the second-hand pair acquired for the lessons. Black hunting coat. Black dress boots. White stock. Bowler. And Marcia Halliday said she thought a veil: "Not entirely appropriate if you're not riding sidesaddle, but it does rather set a gel off." Marcia herself did ride sidesaddle, on occasion, and was definitely set off by the veil, haughtily handsome, like some Trollope heroine.

More expense. Alarming expense, but needs must. The season came. Pam was launched, shepherded by Marcia, instructed to the hilt: always keep your horse's heels away from the hounds, don't barge at gates—wait your turn, never get ahead of the huntsmen or the whippers-in, on a run . . . (as if that were likely).

In fact, as Pam soon discovered, a day out with the hounds was mainly spent standing around with fifty other riders at the side of some copse, while baying sounds came occasionally from within. Or proceeding slowly along a lane, jostled by fifty different riders. With any luck, you could avoid anything more alarming than a brief canter across a plowed field. She never saw a fox. Marcia Halliday would sometimes disappear, and return exhilarated, having been in at a death: "Never mind, Pam—I'm afraid you missed that run. Another time. Willow rather pulled up after that last sighting, didn't he?"

Willow was no more keen than Pam on a good gallop. By tea time, he had his eye on home, his stable, and the cleaning-up process, no doubt pleasurable for him, hard work for Pam. The rubbing down of steaming flanks, the scrubbing of the tack, dunking of the bridle in a bucket of cold water, scrub and scrub, work with saddle soap on the saddle and all leather. It took ages. All to be done immediately, in the dark winter evening, with aching limbs, before you could collapse into a hot bath. Frances, Clare and Imogen would hover, help, anxious for a report.

Actually, it wasn't going too badly at all. Pam had been noticed. Quite right too—tallish, slim, good figure, she looked very well in the beautifully cut cream jodhpurs from Harry Hall (expensive trip to London), perfectly fitting black coat, crisp white stock, and the bowler and veil. On only her second day with the South Devon, hanging around a copse with a group of others, young James Pinnock, son of a big local gentleman farmer, edged his horse alongside her. "Haven't seen you out before. James— James Pinnock. New to the South Devon, are you?"

Pam introduced herself, shyly. She admitted herself new to hunting, indeed. That seemed to go down rather well. James Pinnock became masterful, protective. He instructed her on hound lore—"I'm not boring you, am I? Rotten scent today—we shan't get much of a run." He produced a silver flask from his pocket, took a swig, wiped the mouth carefully with a remarkably clean handkerchief, offered it to Pam.

Pam took a sip of brandy, giggled, handed the flask back. The giggle gave her pink cheeks, behind the veil. James Pinnock gleamed at her, above his red coat—fresh-faced, confident, established, scion of Devon soil. "Good show. See you out next week, I hope."

And then there were others. The Master's son, who helped her to mount again after Willow had stumbled at a bank and unseated her. "Clumsy fellow, he wasn't giving you a thought. Here, you need a knee up . . . I'm Tony Bateman. I don't think we've met?" And Adrian Slope, twenty-eight-year-old ex-Army, son of Sir John and Lady, who got chatting to her outside yet another copse. Quite a long chat.

The pinnacle of the season was of course the Hunt Ball. To which Frances had given much thought. She learned that you went to the Ball in a party, by convention, though once there things would become more of a free-for-all. The convening of the party was a major problem, and in the end she managed to do no better than herself and Ted, with the vet and his wife, Mr. and Mrs. Culver, and their seventeen-year-old son Gordon, mired in sullen adolescence, radiant with acne, but he would have to do as a partner for Pam. To start off with.

And, in the event, it was the Hunt Ball that did it. Pam danced the first dance with Gordon Culver (rigid, treading on her feet). Tony Bateman asked her for the next. And then James Pinnock demanded her. For the next, and the next. Gordon Culver spent the evening sitting at the side, staring at his shoes and wanting to go home. Pam danced and danced. With James Pinnock. Slow foxtrots, cheek to cheek, the lights down now.

The engagement was announced six weeks later. The Pinnocks were perhaps not too thrilled with the match—Devon nabobs farming five hundred acres—but declared gallantly that Pam was an awfully nice girl. Contemplation of the wedding was a matter of anguish for Frances. Expense, expense—how could it be done, on an appropriate scale? The Pinnocks, however, had summed up the situation: a financial imbalance, unfortunately, between the families, but they did not propose to lose face locally with a skimped affair. A tactful word was had with Frances: they would be chipping in, substantially.

The wedding was a delight. Mrs. Bennet could relax, a little: one down, two to go.

Clare took over Willow. Married Pam had available any horse that she wished, and in any case she was rather phasing herself off the hunting field, to concentrate on life as landed gentry; she was to have her own bantam-rearing unit—so sweet, bantams. Absence from the hunting field would in the long run prove to be a bit of a mistake, leaving James a soft target for other men's bored and predatory wives, but that lay in the future.

Clare and Willow set to, next season. They both knew what to do: stick with the crowd, hang around copses, lanes, gates, and with careful management all but the briefest dash across a field could be avoided. Seize every opportunity to be noticed, to get chatting. Clare too looked well in the black hunting coat, altered to fit.

Off the hunting field, Clare had struck up an acquaintance with Jane, a girl her own age whose parents were both local schoolteachers. Jane did not hunt; she appeared surprised at the idea of hunting. Jane was going to Oxford. This, in turn, startled Frances. She couldn't see the point of Oxford, for a girl. Except, she remembered wistfully, for the men. There would be loads of men—you'd be spoiled for choice. In a wild moment she wondered if possibly Immy . . . No, no, that was outlandish.

The hunting season proceeded: mud, rain, frost, snow. The aching limbs, the harness-room housework. The gradual accretion of young men who greeted Clare, and with whom she exchanged pleasantries.

It has to be said that she did not do as well as Pam had done. David Hammond's father was the major estate agent in the area—well-regarded local figure, but perhaps not quite top-drawer. While Frances was just a touch disappointed, you do not disparage a bird in the hand, and the Hammonds had this lovely little manor house all lined up for the couple.

Another wedding.

Just sometimes, Frances felt an odd kind of unease, disquiet, as though there were some faint seismic shudder from her known world, known assumptions, known expectations. That Jane girl, with her Oxford. A cousin's daughter, Pam's age, who was working in the BBC. An old school friend of Pam's who was in Paris, doing a course at the university there.

And then there was Immy.

Immy had embarked on the hunting season, but with evident reluctance. Immy had become a bit—well, bolshy. She had lost the traditional compliance of the Landon girls, and argued about things. Had opinions. Refused to wear a nice skirt and twinset all the time and acquired a pair of slacks. Insisted that they take a real newspaper, other than Daddy's *Sporting Times*. She read it. Wasn't interested in the royal family. Dragged her feet when asked to help Mummy with the flowers. Kept getting books from the local library. Said she wished she'd done Higher School Cert. Smoked.

And then, halfway through the season, she said she wasn't hunting anymore. She hated hunting. I know what it's all about, Mummy, she said, and I'm sorry, but it isn't going to work, for me.

Frances remonstrated, sighed, admonished.

"But, Immy, darling, what will you *do*?"

Immy had that all arranged, it seemed. Sue Tallant who drove the Mobile Library was in desperate need of a voluntary helper (possibly paid a bit, in due course). "*So* interesting," said Immy. "Helping people choose books. And we'll be going all over the place—up on the moor, everywhere."

Frances had not, of course, meant "What will you *do*?" in this narrow, practical sense. She had had the wider vision in mind: strategy, the essential goal. She sighed. "Yes, dear," she said. "I see." Sue Tallant was a nice enough woman. In her forties—competent, confident. Not married.

That seismic shift again. What was going on here? Why was Immy flouting the obvious procedure? The successful procedure—she had only to look at her sisters.

During the next months Immy and the Mobile Library trekked to and fro across the county—to villages and hamlets, up rutted tracks to isolated farms, to cottages where lived one old lady, up over the moor, down into the combes. The library always got through, rain or shine; books—the essential lifeblood. Immy learned librarian skills; she learned also what in years to come would be called people skills—how to steer one client toward a good travel book, identify a thriller they had not read for another, coax the old boy who couldn't see a thing he fancied.

People abounded. Books are essentially a social medium. After a while, Immy had friends and acquaintances hither and thither—a range, a revelation of people, often quite unlike those among whom she had grown up. She felt interestingly untethered; she found that society is much more expansive, more flexible than she had ever realized.

She got to know Bruce Weatherspoon in the pub at Exford, where she and Sue would sometimes stop off for a lunch break. He was working behind the bar, an occasional day job that helped support his real work as a stonemason. Immy had felt awkward at first about going into a pub (I mean, women on their own don't, do they?), but Sue had no such inhibitions, and soon it became entirely normal—locals nodding a greeting. And Bruce Weatherspoon.

Bruce had been to art college in Bristol. His father was a blacksmith, so this was something of a departure, but welcomed by his parents. So Bruce too was Devon born and bred, but at the other end of the spectrum from James Pinnock.

As Immy was well aware. At first, their meetings were clandestine. Bruce had an old rattletrap of a car, and would pick Immy up at the edge of the village, well away from her home, and take her to his cottage, where he had his studio, and she would watch in fascination as he worked on a headstone, an inscription, a memorial.

By the time Immy took Bruce to meet her parents she and he had decided on the future. "I can't tell them this time," she said. "Not right away. My mother may guess, anyway."

Mrs. Bennet did, but without the rejoicing that you would have expected (mission achieved . . .). Frances and Ted Landon received Bruce together, Ted so befuddled with brandy that he was vaguely under the impression that this was a chap about some plumbing problem, Frances speechless with surprise that morphed into dismay. Immy's face told her everything. That, and her ease with this person, this young man with beaming, ruddy face, work-calloused hands, and speech that . . . The West Country accent is charming, of course, but not . . . not on the lips of a potential son-in-law.

Immy and Bruce were married in Exford church, with a small gathering after in the village hall. Frances smiled and endured. Pam and Clare attended; and their husbands, visibly uncomfortable.

So that was that. In due course, Frances would enjoy her grandchildren; some more than others—Immy's children were, well, brought up rather differently. The 50s arrived, and the 60s; Devon still slumbered, perhaps, but elsewhere things were on the move. Girls were now women, and had their own ideas. Marriage held out, but as a choice, not a given. And so the century proceeded, to a time when the shade of Mrs. Bennet would be laid to rest, except perhaps in some moribund enclave of the upper classes.

And from somewhere, many decades ahead, in a further century, a sensitive ear might have been able to pick up a clarion call, the emphatic tone of Immy's great-great-great-granddaughter, Britain's second woman prime minister.

# Lorna and Tom

They were on the seat above the rose garden, with the view over to the lawns beyond, and then Oxfordshire rolling away into hazy distance. Lunch was over, served by the Portuguese couple, Carlos and Maria—just them, Lorna and Tom, and Lorna's parents —and Lorna felt it had gone well. Now Tom seemed rather quiet.

She was on edge. She knew she was falling in love with him.

He said, "I hadn't quite realized . . ."

"Realized what?"

He gestured. At the view, back toward the house. "That you live like this."

She was taken aback. "Oh . . . I'm sorry."

He laughed. "You can't help it. It's hardly your fault."

Then he kissed her.

It was 1956, when the world was young. When she was young, so the world was too—new-minted, just for her. Full of surprises, and he was the best one yet. The young man here with her today, first time at her home. Tom. Tom Clark.

She had met him at her school friend Eleanor's twenty-first birthday party. Eleanor's brother was at London University, and had brought along a bunch of his friends, one of whom was Tom. Lorna had noticed him at once—nice-looking, those brown eyes (noticing her, too, she saw), always smiling and laughing. He asked her to dance, once, twice, and then again and again—smoochy dancing to the radiogram in Eleanor's parents' drawing room, with the carpets rolled back. He was reading English at the university, though he'd rather wanted to go to art college, but his parents weren't keen on that; he lived in Enfield. That was about all she learned that night; he asked for her phone number. A week or so later, they went to a film together, with tea at a Kardomah before. A few days later, a walk by the river, in the evening, with London glittering all around them. His father was a primary school teacher, she now knew; Tom would probably go into teaching himself. They held hands, and both knew that this was the beginning.

And now he was here, at her home, for the weekend. Her mother had already murmured that he seemed a nice boy. Daddy hadn't said anything.

Her father made washing powder. His factory made it—Braithwaites. Factories—the other one too that made bleach and stuff like that. Lorna was never sure exactly what they did; it was all a bit of a joke—"Daddy's cleaning things." But the cleaning things that, yes, sort of paid for everything—the lovely home outside Henley with the huge garden and the tennis court and the swimming pool, and her ponies that she was long since bored with, and her boarding school and the finishing school in Switzerland and now her car, a super cream-colored Ford Consul.

\*

Somewhere else, in another time, she waits for him. Lunch. The Criterion in Piccadilly. Later, she will meet a friend at the Royal Academy, to see the exhibition there. She always needs to do something, after. Be busy.

\*

He was quite quiet, that weekend. On best behavior, she knew. Among his friends he was different. She had seen him now with others, established as his girl, and saw him as popular, gregarious, always up for some fun. But it was his third year at the university, and he was working hard. They couldn't see each other all that often. She would come up to London and they'd have an hour or two together, or she would drive up and they'd go out to Epping Forest or somewhere. A few of his friends might come on these jaunts, piling in, girls sitting on someone's knee. None of them had a car; they called Lorna's "the jalopy": "So where are we going in the jalopy this evening?"

She was never entirely at ease with these university friends. Especially the girls, though there weren't that many—far more men than girls. But the few that Tom knew were a coterie, and Lorna knew she could never be part of it. They talked about getting jobs at the BBC, or on newspapers. Lorna was wise enough not to mention the Domestic Science course that she was doing—a couple of days a week. Those girls were polite enough to her, but with a politeness that was not particularly welcoming. She felt tolerated, merely, by all Tom's friends, because she was his girl, and her car was a convenience. She said as much to him once. He protested that no, no, they really like you, it's just that we've all known each other ages now and you're . . . different.

But it was about to finish, his immersion in that comfortable camaraderie. The term ended, and with it Tom's time at the university. Now they could meet frequently, in town, or driving out into the country somewhere. Tom got a part-time job at a market garden; in the autumn he would start his PGCE—teacher training course. And during that long idyllic summer everything firmed up between them. For Lorna, it was an ecstatic today, but she saw tomorrow unreeling ahead, unthinkable yet imaginable. Being with him all the time, a home of their own, perhaps one day children.

She explained to him that he would have to speak to her father. Ask him. They couldn't just tell Daddy that they were going to get married. So, on another weekend at her home, Tom went to Harold Braithwaite's study and had this conversation with him.

Lorna wanted to know every word. "And then what did he say?"

"He said that for obvious reasons he wasn't going to ask me if I was in a position to be able to support you." Tom laughed—an uneasy laugh. Lorna understood that he had had a hard time. Well, Daddy was like that. People said that was why he was so successful in business.

"I'm trying to work that out. Meaning—he sees my earning potential as not so great, or, *you* can perfectly well be self-supporting?"

"But was he . . . pleased?" She was anxious, now.

"Well, he didn't say no."

"But what else?"

"He said: I must assume that Lorna knows what she wants."

Oh, she did, she did. She wanted Tom, now and for always, his smile, his laugh, his capacity for fun, his energy, the way he looked at her, as no one had ever looked before.

It was a big wedding. Both she and Tom would have preferred something on a lesser scale, but for Lorna's mother it was a once-in-a-lifetime event, and her father needed to invite a fair number of his business friends. So there was the wedding in St. James's Piccadilly, with a flock of small relatives as bridesmaids, and the reception for two hundred at the Savoy. Lorna was in a daze, but alert enough to keep an eye out for Tom's parents, who were going to find the occasion a bit of an ordeal. She had met them several times now, taken by Tom to the little house in Enfield.

It had seemed very small, the first time she went. It occurred to her that she had never before been inside one of those semi-detacheds you see everywhere, lining every suburban road. The sitting-room almost filled up by the three-piece suite; the

dining room with the hatch through to the kitchen; the rect-
angle of garden beyond. She sat there awkwardly, that first time,
aware that her own home was of a different order—the size, the
furnishings, its emphatic footprint—and uneasily conscious that
Tom must have told his parents this. But they were really nice—
his father rather like Tom, warm and funny, you could tell what
a good teacher he must be. And she saw at once that these were
people entirely comfortable with their lives—settled, positive,
engaged with a world she did not know. Tom's mother was welcoming, talkative—quite direct, she could be. On another
occasion, when Lorna was helping her with the washing-up, she
said, "You and Tom, you've known very different circumstances.
Is that going to be a problem?" Then at once she laughed, and
patted Lorna's arm: "Silly question. You can rise above that, both
of you. Glasses go in the top cupboard, Lorna, and that jug lives
on the dresser." She was small and quick; she worked in a Citi-
zens Advice Bureau— you knew she would be briskly efficient.
Lorna knew also that she would seem entirely alien to her own
mother, for whom a busy day was a visit to the hairdresser and
lunch with a friend.

Eventually, after the engagement and with the wedding plans
in full swing, his parents came to lunch at Willow Court. Lorna
was on edge, conscious as never before of the trappings, the
insidious presence of Maria and Carlos, the yawning space of the
drawing room, the parquet floor, the Persian rugs, the old oil
paintings on the walls, her mother's flower arrangements, the
sense of comfort and largesse. She had never thought of her
home like this before; it had redefined itself, at the same time
familiar and disconcertingly alternative.

But the Clarks did not seem disconcerted. They made no com-
ments (later, Lorna's mother said, "She didn't seem really to notice
the rose garden"), talked easily, listened in attentive silence

to the account of the wedding arrangements ("I'd thought they'd be rather thrilled at the idea of the Savoy, but they didn't say anything"). After, Lorna asked Tom if he thought it had gone off all right.

He smiled. "My parents tend to take things in their stride." All the same, Lorna had felt a bit apprehensive, where the wedding was concerned. So many people they wouldn't know—wouldn't get on with, really. She saw to it that they were seated with Tom's friends, sought out her godmother to talk to them, a person who wouldn't—well, be heavy-handed, patronizing.

*

In that other time, another world, she takes out her phone to check there is no message, then sneaks a glance in her mirror. When she looks up, she sees him at the far end of the restaurant, handing his coat to an attendant. She straightens, firms up a smile.

*

The house in Chelsea was the wedding present from her father. When eventually one day Lorna looked at the deeds, putting them away in a safe place, she saw that they were in her name only. She hadn't ever thought about that, and made sure that Tom did not see them.

Tom had intended to continue with his teacher training course, which would have meant a seriously curtailed honeymoon in Italy (present from Lorna's godmother). Lorna had quite a job to persuade him to postpone starting it, but eventually he agreed, and that was good because it meant he was around to help when they settled into the house and also that he had time to do his own thing. Tom was quite talented artistically; he could draw and paint well, and now he found a place locally where you could learn to pot, and he was getting rather good at that. He joined the Chelsea Arts Club, and met up with a group of congenial people there.

They were good years, those first two, three, married years. Lorna was, quite simply, happy. She had not been unhappy before—home was fine, her parents were fine, mostly—but this was contentment of another dimension. Tom's enhancing presence, all the time, his love, the sense of being, now, the two of them, the house that it was such fun to furnish and furbish. Her father had made new arrangements; the allowance that she had had since she was sixteen was replaced with a trust fund. He explained the income that this would produce, briskly, in one of those conversations in his study. She had said: "It seems such a lot, Daddy."

Harold Braithwaite's reply was terse: "I think you'll find you need it."

She knew that Tom felt awkward that he was contributing nothing. She had set up a joint bank account on which he could draw for any needs; he was frugal to a degree with this, resisting buying new clothes, having to be chivied into getting the art materials he wanted, into paying for the pottery course. Gradually, it seemed that he got more used to the situation and their little arguments about it stopped. Once, she had said: "It's only money, Tom. Just money. It doesn't matter." And he had put his arms round her, rubbed his cheek against hers—a bristly cheek, it was, he was experimenting with a beard: "You're such an innocent, sweetie, and I love you for it."

The 1950s became 1960, bringing some sort of new dawn, Lorna felt, the new decade in which she was still young, but a young mother, because she was pregnant now, waiting serenely in the Chelsea house for this confirmation of married life. Tom was waiting too, conveniently to hand most of the time because the top floor of the house had been converted into a studio for him; he had his easels there, his painting equipment. The teacher training course hadn't worked out; the place was right out at Enfield, near his parents' home, a terrible slog to get there day after day. Lorna had felt it was such a pity he had so little time to do what he really liked doing, now that he had the studio . . . "And were you so absolutely *sure* about teaching, anyway?" Tom had reflected, staring out of the studio window at the rooftops of Chelsea, expensive rooftops even now, and due to become even more so. He had said that maybe not, you've got a point, maybe not . . . But that all this—he gestured at the paints and brushes, the canvases, the paraphernalia of the studio—all this can seem a touch self-indulgent.

"Oh, no," she had cried. "Oh, no, darling, you're so good at it."

He frowned, then laughed. "Quite good. Just quite good."

She admired what he did. The swirly landscapes, lovely strong colors—quite like Graham Sutherland. And the portraits—sort of impressionist, but he really caught the person. One of his landscapes hung now at Willow Court; her mother had loved it—insisted on buying it though of course Tom wanted it to be a present.

His parents had one too. They had gone on at him rather about the teacher training course, at first, but seemed to have given up now. They did not often visit the Chelsea house, both of them so busy, of course, but Lorna's mother was often there, and even more so after Christine was born. She thought Lorna was so amazing to be managing without any sort of help, not even an au pair.

Lorna had found that a baby was something she could do, rather to her surprise. She didn't mind the broken nights, the disruption, the constrictions on her own life. She loved the new status; she wore Christine like some kind of badge of honor.

Two years later, Christine was joined by Charles. Lorna had been determined that Christine should not be an only, as she herself had been. And one more . . . she thought privately, not mentioning this to Tom. Tom had taken easily to fatherhood, relished the children, showed them off to his friends at the Arts Club. He spent quite a lot of evenings there, but did not so much bring people to the house. Lorna always found herself at a loss with the Arts Club lot; they weren't all artists, not real artists, but did creative things, in advertising, publishing. The girls— well, young women they all were now—had glitzy jobs, hectic lives. It was clear that they saw Christine and Charles not so much as status symbols, badges of honor, but as albatrosses round Lorna's neck. "Poor *you*," they said. "But you're so marvelous with them."

The 1960s were well and truly launched. People like this—the Arts Club lot, everyone in Chelsea, indeed—were nicely in tune with the Zeitgeist, but Lorna was not. She wore miniskirts—of course, you had to; she had her hair cut short, but those mascara-drenched eyes were not for her. She never had worn much make-up. As for clothes—she conformed, up to a point; once, in a fit of nostalgia, she put on a Pringle twin-set and a tweed skirt she found lurking at the back of a cupboard. Tom laughed and laughed; she hadn't really meant it as a joke.

He was painting and drawing a fair amount, but was also involved now with a craft co-operative, helping to promote the work, arrange exhibitions. Lorna was quite glad of this, although it meant he was away from time to time; it gave him a purpose, she could see. He had had one small exhibition of his own work, and quite a few things had sold. When she had been celebratory about this he had pulled a face: "Yes, and all bought by friends or relatives."

She took the children a lot to Willow Court; they needed the space, the garden, the swimming pool. The Chelsea house was beginning to feel quite small, especially when there was a new baby—Paula—and Lorna finally had to give in and take on an au pair girl. After that, girls came and went—the Biancas and

Ingrids and Solanges; toddlers morphed into children, there was exponential growth of their requirements, schools and dancing and swimming and music and football, and it was all fine, Lorna found. She could do this too, like she had found she could do babies. And she had an occupation; she was necessary, essential.

In 1968 Lorna's mother died: a treacherous unnoticed tumor, inoperable. Lorna was desolate, and then anxiously protective of her father. But he was plunged ever more into work; he had recently taken over another business, there were now two more factories, and he was forever on the move between them, or in his London office. Willow Court remained a base, and available, manned by the Portuguese couple, but somehow lifeless. Harold Braithwaite used his London flat more and more. He visited the Chelsea house occasionally.

"This won't do, really," he said, one day, looking round.

Lorna was surprised. "But we love it, Daddy. Though I suppose we are filling it up rather, now."

The Gloucestershire house, when all was signed and sealed, and the building work completed, had a studio for Tom at the end of the garden. He had joined Lorna in the house-hunting, rather silent, sometimes. Lorna explained that naturally they'd still be in the London house, this was just for weekends and school holidays. She couldn't account for what seemed not exactly lack of enthusiasm on his part, but some kind of detachment, as though it were not really his concern.

But, as time passed, Tom was more and more at the Gloucestershire house. He seemed to have drifted apart from his Arts Club friends, and began to get together with what Lorna thought of as "arty" people in the country. It was surprising how many potters there were about, painters, sculptors, and those who practiced one craft or another. Tom was not painting much; he worked for a while with a local furniture maker, and sought now to make elegant pieces himself—the studio became a carpentry center.

When Christine and Charles, in turn, went to boarding school, Lorna made the decision that Gloucestershire should now become their main home. There was a nice little private day school not far away that Paula could go to, until she too began to board, a moment that Lorna dreaded.

"Then don't," said Tom. "Send her to the local comprehensive. Send them all, for that matter."

He spoke, as so often these days, as though it were not really his concern. And when Lorna said that well, yes, I mean it would be fine by me, but Daddy would be simply horrified, I couldn't do that to him, Tom shrugged.

Presently Christine was joined at Westonbirt by Paula; Lorna did rather like them being at her own old school. The thought somehow mitigated the loss that she felt: the empty house, for weeks on end, until, thanks be, they all came tumbling back for the holidays. But those barren weeks were hard to get through. She determinedly sought occupation—some voluntary work at a hospice, a course in garden design. She would redo the garden entirely, get Tom involved in choices, decisions. He left everything to her too much, she felt: "Whatever you prefer, darling . . . Whichever you like . . ."

*

And here he is, provoking, as always, a sudden lurch in her composure. They greet, he sits down. For a few minutes they engage in chitchat, but this does not go on for long. They have an agenda today: they need to talk about a shared concern. Paula: Paula's impending divorce.

*

The 1970s did not much leave their mark on rural Gloucestershire. Some flared jeans, some cheesecloth shirts—Lorna herself wore a long wrap-around skirt—but not much by way of attitudes or assumptions. Tom's friends—the potters, the craftspeople—were long since dedicated to creativity, and when the urge to demonstrate a creative flair became a widespread fashion, they could show benign contempt. This would pass, and did, along with the sideburns and the tie-dyeing.

Indeed, Tom's own sideburns came and went, but he was now quite respectably involved in furniture-making; original designs executed in oak and elm—the studio had to be expanded. He sold pieces at craft fairs, and insisted on using the proceeds to contribute to the costs of the studio extension, though Lorna knew he needed anything that came in for materials. He had long since ceased to quibble about drawing on their joint account, but did so meticulously, mentioning to Lorna any unusual expenditure.

"But you don't need to *tell* me, darling."

"I know, I know—it's only money." An odd sort of smile, one that always bothered her, somehow.

Christine left school and went to university, followed in due course by Charles. They still came home a fair amount, of course, but Lorna could see yawning ahead that time when they would not. There was talk already of possible futures: Charles might do postgraduate work in America, Christine wanted a London job. Well, there would be Paula for a while yet; Lorna clung to that thought. She was worried by the idea of there just being her and Tom at home.

It was not that there was anything wrong between them, she told herself: no, no. More that there was this absence of anything much at all. They shared a bed at night, and yes, Tom still made love to her (well, sometimes, and middle-aged people just don't so much, do they?); by day he vanished into his studio or off to some craft fair or to visit friends, associates she did not know, never suggesting she came too ("Oh, you'd be bored, darling, it's all just talk about stuff we do").

And so, when it happened, she was not prepared, was not expecting it, was ambushed.

When he came into the kitchen one day and said, "Lorna, can we have a talk?"

She was cooking for the freezer. Paula was home from university; Christine was coming for the weekend.

They sat down, opposite sides of the kitchen table. Lorna looked at him. She saw the Tom she had known for twenty-four years, and understood that she hadn't.

He told her that it wasn't working, was it? That it had not been working for a long time, possibly it never really had, and they had not faced up to this. He told her that yes, he had loved her, and that there was a sense in which he still did, but that he couldn't stay with her. He was sorry, he said, really, really sorry, but that he had to do this, should maybe have done it earlier, but couldn't while the children were young. He said they might understand, now. He hoped, desperately, that she might.

She said she didn't.

No, he said, no. There wasn't anyone else. That, she believed.

Stricken, she fell silent. And, a while later, Tom moved out.

The divorce went ahead. Lorna's father said, "Lawyers are trying to tell me he's entitled to a percentage of this, a percentage of that. Well, we'll fight—he's not getting a penny."

There was no need to fight. Tom asked for nothing. Just the contents of his studio.

In the years to come Lorna never questioned the children for news of him, but learned some, nevertheless. The children had their own lives now, and she knew that these included time spent with their father. He was in Somerset, in business partnership with another furniture-maker—less high-end products, she understood, more by way of mass production, they were doing quite well.

In time, she heard of Annie, whom Tom had met apparently through his business partner, some relative of his, and in more time still she heard that they were married. This shook her, left her stricken again, for a while. But then she began to see George Wheatley, whose wife had died, who farmed vast tracts of Gloucestershire and was so easy to get on with, and that helped. Much of the time.

Enough to fall into this practice of meeting up with Tom every year or so. A drink, a lunch. To talk about the children, mostly. Occasions that Lorna both dreaded and looked for.

*

As, indeed, today. But, in fact, nowadays she is pretty calm about it. Here we are again, she thinks, and goodness, how can he have got quite so—well, quite so old. As am I, but I know about that because I see this face in the mirror every day. But Tom . . . The Tom in her head is twenty-two still—one of the many Toms in her head.

They discuss Paula. "It's just so sad," says Lorna. "Such a pity. I'd thought they were happy together. I like Matthew."

Tom sighs. He says that he too is surprised, but there it is. He is concerned about Zoe, the child, their grandchild. Zoe is six.

Lorna too is worried. "Going from one to the other, it seems. Oh dear, I hate to think of that for her." Couldn't they have hung in there, for Zoe's sake? After all, Tom . . . She is thinking now of their own marriage, she realizes. And perhaps Tom is also, because a silence falls between them. A weighted silence, and both look away, avoid each other's eye.

It is Tom who speaks first, acknowledging what is in the air. "One can't make comparisons," he says. "We can't know what they . . . how they . . . We were . . ."

"We were what?" says Lorna.

"Different." He looks away again. "Well, of course"—shaking his head—"that's stupid. Let's not go there, Lorna."

And then Lorna says it, that which she has never said before.

"What went wrong?" she says. "What went wrong between you and me?"

He does look at her now. He takes a breath.

"You were rich, Lorna," he says. "Just that. You were rich."

# Point of View

The Scriptwriter is wrestling with the question of POV. Point of View. She has these three characters shut up in a room together, engaged in a discussion which must reveal, at the same time, their relationships with one another, aspects of their individual histories, and the current state of play in all three lives. To do this, she needs to display the scene from different points of view. The characters in question are in the nineteenth century. This is a costume drama series—it is hoped that it will trounce *Downton Abbey*. So there is the added complication of the nineteenth-century POV, which does not come naturally to the Scriptwriter but must be seamlessly suggested.

The Scriptwriter is Lauren Stanley, and right now, as she sits at her desk, wrestling, everything is seen from her POV. The screen of the laptop in front of her, the view of the street out of the window above. And, especially, thoughts which are distracting her from work, thoughts about a real-life connection which keep shoving aside these fictional concerns. She is a bit—well, quite a lot—worried about her relationship with her partner, Paul. It occurs to her that real life is a single POV affair, or rather, a matter of myriad conflicting POVs.

The relationship is not in crisis, but in poor health. It has a bad case of flu, from which it may well recover, but it is in need of care and attention. Lauren thinks of it in that way, as though it were some delicate substance—the Relationship. She is concerned about it.

Is Paul concerned?

Ah—this is where POV comes in. She does not know if Paul is concerned, if he is aware that things are not good, or, if he is aware, whether he is concerned. Or just not bothered, possibly. Is he thinking: so we're not getting on . . . well—whatever.

Paul is a research chemist. He works for a big pharmaceutical company. A pharma, you say nowadays. His work is about as remote from Lauren's as could be, a matter of substances and reactions, hypotheses and results. No nonsense about what he said or she said or who did what, when, where and to whom. No hint of a POV.

They met at the wedding of a mutual friend. Oh, cliché, cliché. Met, got talking, took a shine to one another, met up a week later, took further shine, the gulf between their occupations no impediment whatsoever, met up again, and again, went to bed, went to Venice for a weekend, were spoken of as a couple, moved in together. Lauren, Paul, Harry and Archie.

Harry is Paul's thirteen-year-old son. Archie is Lauren's cat. Paul has been married (he is somewhat older than Lauren)—Harry is the detritus of the marriage and is actually only with them alternate weekends and some of the school holidays, though it sometimes seems longer than that to Lauren. When she and Paul first got together Harry was a charming—well, mainly charming—six-year-old. Thirteen is less charming. Most of Harry's time is spent with his mother, who lives in Maidenhead, and exerts a malign influence from there.

Archie is a ten-year-old neutered tabby. He has had no previous relationship.

Lauren has. Two. Eighteen months and three years. She has been assuming for some time that she and Paul are a fixture, which is why the Relationship's onset of flu is a worry. She considers the symptoms each day, testing them for progress. Better? Or worse?

Paul fails frequently to give her that quick kiss before he goes off to work.

He seldom inquires about *her* work, which he used to do.

Sex, when it happens, feels perfunctory.

All that is worse.

Better was when he did remember her birthday. When he and Harry brought a choice takeaway supper back for them all after they had been to a football match. When he reached out for her hand in the car last week.

But worse are all these times he has nothing to say. When he comes home late (could he be having an affair?). When he seems not to care whether she is around or not.

She does not really think he is having an affair. Paul just is not that sort of man (but anyone could suddenly become that sort of man, couldn't they, if subject to a *coup de foudre*?). And he hates crisis, upheaval. The end of his first marriage shattered him. That Relationship suffered some kind of terminal flu, it seems. He prefers not to talk about it.

The Scriptwriter homes in on her three characters, determinedly. She has one of them move to the fireplace, and turn angrily to her sister saying . . . Saying what?

Lauren wonders if Paul really has these departmental meetings that make him late home—very late—every Tuesday. He probably does. Paul is deeply involved in his work. This is a much more likely scenario than some woman tucked up in an adulterous flat.

The Scriptwriter frowns, stares at her screen, types: "Charlotte (angrily): That is untrue, Emily. I have never spoken ill of you—I have *not*, I have *not*."

Lauren compares life with Paul now to life with Paul, say, a year ago. Surely he talked to her more then? Surely sex was more enthusiastic? There was more companionship: going to see a film, a walk in the park. Last weekend he didn't want to come for a walk with her, stayed home reading the paper.

The Scriptwriter tells Emily to reply. Emily is silent.

Lauren sifts the last week for some positively companionable, even affectionate, moment. Paul patted her on the shoulder when asking what was for supper. An e-mail he sent from the office to say what time he would be home had a couple of Xs at the end. He has never been one for endearments, so absence of a "darling" or two means nothing.

The Scriptwriter sighs, closes the screen, and consigns her characters to the depths of the laptop.

Lauren considers their respective personalities; pronounced differences are perhaps relevant. She knows that she is more volatile, more excitable, more prone to panic or dismay. None of these defects are present to excess, but they are not reflected in Paul's personality. Paul is phlegmatic. He is even-tempered, inclined to caution, rational, conscientious, persistent.

So, given what seems a certain apposition, is she just fussing? Is it just that Paul doesn't react like she does, so seems distant?

No. Because if always a bit calm and cool he has become more so. Much more so.

Are they an otherwise mismatched couple? Paul is tall, gangly, with a long thin face, glasses. Lauren is short, inclined to plump, with (she considers) a reasonable face, quite pretty even, perfect eyesight.

No, appearance is irrelevant.

Are their living circumstances unsatisfactory? Well, not really. They moved into the Finsbury Park flat three years ago, after a prolonged engagement with London house prices, and are very pleased with it; their bedroom, a small one for Harry, Lauren's study, sitting room, bathroom, kitchen with high cabinet on top of which Archie usually roosts, paws neatly folded, surveying them. No, the flat is fine.

Problems with their extended families? Paul's mother is widowed; Lauren gets on well with her, they visit regularly, Eileen comes to them for Christmas. His only sibling, a sister, lives in Australia but relations have been entirely amicable on her occasional visits.

Lauren also has a sister, of whom she is fond. Paul has always seemed to like her well enough, and her husband. Sally recently had her second child, and Lauren was careful, when last she and Paul went there, to refrain from any enthusiastic reaction or comment; no "Oh, isn't he lovely!," no pleas to be allowed to hold him. Indeed, she remembers making some breezy remark on the way home to the effect that Sally was in danger of becoming a complete baby bore: "Rather her than me!"

Paul does not want them to have a child together. His silence on the matter has made that clear to Lauren.

Lauren is thirty-six. Before too long it would be too late anyway. So she has bitten the bullet, told herself if that is the way it is, then that's the way it is, get over it, get a life.

No, families pose no problems. And the baby issue . . . The baby issue is her problem; she has never confronted Paul, sensing how he feels, never made anything of it, has not risked wrecking this good, solid relationship. He has Harry—well, a share of Harry; she can understand that that is enough, for him.

And she has her work, her absorbing work, which is enough for her, isn't it? She has her work, she has a much-loved partner, she has a choice flat in a sought-after area of London, she has good health, a stable bank balance, and an assertive cat who is winding round her legs right now not out of affection but because he wants food.

Lauren feeds Archie: Whiskas, one pouch.

There, she tells him. You are not a baby substitute, and never were. I am fond of you, but in a perfectly balanced, merely cat-loving way.

Archie eats.

Later, Lauren feeds Paul: chili con carne, followed by a fruit salad.

Paul eats, but with expressed appreciation. Chili con carne is a favorite of his. He pours them each a glass of wine.

Archie, with practiced agility, has leaped to the top of the kitchen cabinet and settled himself, observing them without apparent interest.

Paul has had an exacting day. Now, back home, he is trying to put these things out of his mind and concentrate on . . . chili con carne, a glass of Sauvignon, the sight of Lauren, in that gray stripy top and the amber pendant he gave her for Christmas.

Paul loves Lauren. His POV, right now, is of the person he loves, eating her supper, talking about something someone said in the supermarket. Fine, you might think. What more could a man want?

Except that it is not fine. Not quite. Because there hovers around Lauren an absence. There is something missing. A someone.

Paul knows that Lauren does not want to have a child with him. That is clear from the fact that she has never raised the matter, from the merrily disparaging remarks she makes about her sister's new baby. All right. All right, if that is the way she feels. But for him, there is this hovering absence. This wistful wishing. It has made him a bit offhand with her lately—he knows that.

Lauren says, "I never understand how Archie gets to the top of that cabinet. It would be, for us, like jumping about twenty feet."

"Well," says Paul, "he is differently constructed. Constructed to leap. But yes, it always does seem rather an achievement."

"I've watched him. One jump up onto the counter. Then he sort of eyes the top of the cabinet, and there is this effortless liftoff. And he arrives. If there is reincarnation," Lauren goes on, "I'm coming back as a domestic cat."

"In order to be able to jump on top of kitchen cabinets?"

"Because it's the most luxurious, unthreatened life going. Everything you need supplied. No dangers. Nothing demanded of you."

Paul considers. "Limited, then, one might say. No challenges or achievements—except access to high places."

"That's anthropomorphism. Animals don't think in terms of challenges or achievements. Survival is all. And reproduction, of course. Poor old Archie. Snipped in youth. No genetic drive for him."

"Then he is spared," says Paul.

Something in his voice makes Lauren look more intently at him. "Spared?"

Paul shrugs. "A maddening compulsion, I imagine. Necessitating indiscriminate sexual pursuit and mortal combat with rivals. We're lucky to have more contained feelings."

"Yes," says Lauren. "I suppose we are."

There is a silence. An odd silence, somehow—no, not pregnant, inappropriate word. Loaded, perhaps.

The freight that this silence carries seems to fill the room. A thought freight emanating from him, from her.

Paul thinks of children. Not of specific children, not of his Harry, but of abstract children. The concept of children. The reproductive drive, he supposes sourly. Somehow, it doesn't feel quite like that. It feels less ruthless, more considered, more *human*.

Lauren does not so much think as experience. First, she experiences the baby issue that she thought she had managed to tamp down. It comes surging up: disturbing, dismaying. Then, looking at Paul, she seems to begin to experience something quite different: she is not just looking at Paul but looking out from him. It is as though her POV has suffered fission, and become double. She sees Paul but she also sees herself, a Paul's-eye view of herself, and she understands that she is lacking, that there is an absence, that he wants more of her, that there should be more of her.

"Do you?" she ventures, at last.

"Do I what?"

"Have . . . have feelings that way?"

He gazes at her. He is all POV.

"Well, yes," he says. "I do."

If she could levitate, she would. She would rise up in joy, sail round the room, rejoice, rejoice.

Lauren says, "Actually, me too."

There is a silence. Paul reaches for the wine, fills their glasses. "I had no idea. You've never . . ."

"Said. Nor have you."

"I thought you . . ."

"Didn't want to?" says Lauren. "And I thought *you* didn't."

Paul's expression is a turbulence of surprise, delight, confusion, pleasure. And he is not that kind of man. He is a calm man, phlegmatic. It occurs to Lauren—the Scriptwriter surfaces now, for a moment—that if she were writing this scene the POVs would be rampant, competing.

"I've been *so* . . ." She shakes her head. "So not *realizing*."

"And I'm afraid I've been . . . well, I'd got a bit glum about it."

The POVs, at this point, are no longer rampant but are holding hands, united. And so, too, are Lauren and Paul. Holding hands across the kitchen table, smiling, planning, anticipating.

Archie, perhaps sensitive to a change in kitchen atmosphere, drops down from his perch. But no, he is prompted not by sensibility but opportunism. The pan from which Lauren served the chili con carne is on the side, not entirely empty. And something tells Archie that people are not, right now, paying attention.

Archie eats.

# DIY

Here we go, she thought: "Ripe for renovation." Of course. Another one.

Tim was turning off the main road, responding to the sat nav. They left the traffic, forged through a mesh of suburban streets, arrived at the heart of what had once been a rural village, now digested by later development. Row of old cottages, a pub, the church.

"Should be just along here," he said.

"An irresistible wreck?"

He laughed. Patted her knee. "Trust me."

"No way. Medieval barn, is it?"

"If only. Thirties, I think. Ah—must be this."

He pulled up. They studied the house. Undistinguished. Plain, thought Laura. Basic house. Bit like a child's drawing: front door, window each side, three above. And yes, crack in the brickwork, roof tiles missing, window frames haven't seen a splash of paint in years. Right up Tim's street.

There had been the murky basement flat in Kentish Town. A gleaming space by the time he had done with it, all wood floors and halogen lights and clever cupboards. And the two-up, two-down in Croydon, to which he had given a loft and a conservatory extension. She had never lived other than surrounded by tools and timber and drums of paint. Oh well—he's worth it.

He had the key from the agent, unlocked the door.

"Nice and damp," she said, sniffing.

"Empty for ages, apparently. The price is good. Very good.

And we'd get it down." He was diving into the rooms at either side of the hallway. She heard him banging across the boarded floors, throwing open a window.

Staircase to the side of the hall, up to the floor above, where there was a small landing, with rooms opening off. Steep staircase, surprisingly steep, not well designed.

He had flung open the door at the back of the hall. Kitchen, she saw. Well, sort of kitchen, once.

She joined him. "Just what I've always wanted—granite worktops, cabinet lighting, carving trolley."

He put his arm around her. "You'll get all that. Let's have a look upstairs."

"It's a good thing I love you," she said. "Most women would be out of here and into the car by now."

They climbed the stairs. The wood of the banister was splintered and there were balusters missing. The landing above had a loose plank that lurched when stepped on. Tim opened doors to rooms. "Ah. You'd do an en suite here. Maybe knock another window in this one—a bit dark."

She sighed.

He was inspecting floorboards. "Sand them throughout. Possibly slate flags in the kitchen. Oh . . ." He had spotted a dead bird in the corner of what she now grimly knew would be their bedroom. He picked it up by one desiccated wing and dropped it out of the window.

"Dead birds I can do," she said. "A passing inconvenience. I'm more interested in damp, and that dysfunctional roof, and a funny smell in what is supposed to be a bathroom, and that crack up there, and those over there."

He was leaning out of the window. "Old orchard at the end of the garden. You'd make a paved area—perhaps steps up from it to the lawn. Come and look."

She looked. Shaggy grass. Nettles. Remains of a bonfire. Various plastic bags. The carcass of a child's buggy.

"No one could ever accuse you of lack of imagination," she said.

He grinned. That confiding grin that had first won her, at some party she'd nearly not gone to, eons ago, or so it now seemed. Six years, actually.

"You're on board, then?" he said.

"What choice do I have?"

"You'll love it. Eventually. You'll see."

"Ah. You mean we're going to settle here?"

"Oh, well . . ." He shrugged. "Let's have another poke around the kitchen area."

Down those stairs. Cold, she thought. Extraordinarily cold in here. June day, sun outside, and so cold.

Central heating installation one of his specialties. Just as well.

He was a local government official. Not a builder. He worked in an office, amid computers and filing cabinets, and escaped to his power drill, his saws, his hammers, his larder of screws and nuts and bolts and intricate ironmongery, his drawing board, his pencils and set squares and compasses. Then, he took flight.

Laura taught. She taught six- to seven-year-olds. One day, they would have one of these of their own. Two, maybe. Nice. When he had banged his way through enough decayed properties.

She could stand it—the dust, the dishevelment. In a curious way, she quite liked it, because this was essence of Tim—his energy, his beguiling enthusiasm, the way he flung himself into a new project, on a high with schemes, his eyes alight with power showers and quarry tiles and fitted cupboards. Weekends, she supplied endless cups of tea and coffee, admired, consoled when something went awry. Their outings were to Homebase and builders' merchants. Once, contemplating fireplaces in a reclamation yard, he said, "When you can't put up with any more of this you must say so."

She smiled. "Seriously? And then what will you do with yourself?"

"Crosswords? Sudoku? Learn to play the violin. Take up judo. You are a saint. I know that. You indulge me."

"I suppose it could be said that I am climbing the property ladder. We both are."

"Never thought of it like that. It's the doing it. Do you like this one? Lovely marble surround."

"Exactly. And that's why I indulge you. And no, marble is not appropriate for a small Croydon terrace house."

She loved the intensity of his application, his ability to concentrate for hours on the exact construction of a shelf. He had made a wrought-iron spiral stair for that basement, an exquisite tiled bathroom for the Croydon terrace, squeezed into an extension. Once she had suggested to him quite seriously that he should think of packing in office life and go into business as a builder.

He laughed. "But it's exactly because it's not work. That's the joy of it."

And now, she saw, there would be this somewhat unlovely, seriously dilapidated and enticingly cheap house in an outer London suburb. Oh, well. And it was worth it for his soaring good spirits—always so when on the brink of a new undertaking.

"This is going to be really good. Huge potential. The only thing is, it could take years."

"I shan't complain," she said. "Who knows—you might decide to live in it."

It was autumn when they took possession. Within weeks the ground floor was piled high with his equipment; weekends were spent sourcing materials. Radiators, piping—he was making central heating a priority, thank goodness—timber, tiles. They both had farther to travel to work from here, but even so he would set to each evening, if only to sit staring at squared paper on his clipboard, working out how he would deal with some particular space in the house. He was happy, and she with him. They made love a lot.

The neighbor appeared when they had been there about a month. Elderly woman—eighty plus—coming up the front path, eyeing things as she went: timber under a tarpaulin, that sagging gutter. Laura saw her out of the window and went to the door.

"I've tried you before but you're gone a lot. Sheila Bates. I live down there." The visitor waved toward the nearest housing—a little nineteenth-century terrace beyond the scrubby field that separated their own house from the rest of the sprawling nearby development. Tim was a touch concerned about this field: likely to be built on, at some point. "I see you've builders in. High time someone did some work on the place."

Laura smiled. "The builder isn't a professional, I'm afraid." She hesitated. "I'd suggest a cup of tea, but it's an awful mess in here."

"That'll be all right." Sheila Bates had both feet on the doormat by now anyway: stumpy woman, stick in one hand, Asda carrier bag in the other. "I've not been in here for years. The last people weren't what you'd call matey, and they're long gone anyway."

Laura took her into the kitchen, put the kettle on.

The visitor inspected the room. "Well, he'll have his hands full with this. Dry rot, I shouldn't be surprised. And that roof . . . Nobody's much stayed, and then it's left empty. Children?"

"No," said Laura. "Milk?" Oh, dear. Well, maybe there are other neighbors.

"Yes, and one sugar. Both at work, are you?"

"We are. Have you lived here long?"

Sheila Bates became more expansive. Since childhood, it seemed. Born here, left for elsewhere to marry, husband died.

Parents also, twenty years ago. "And then I thought I'd sooner end up here than in Manchester where we'd gone. So I'm back where I began." She fished in the Asda bag. "Here—green tomato chutney. Made it last week."

Laura took the jar, thanking effusively. There, heart of gold after all.

"Doing heating, is he? Those radiators out there? You'll need it. That him outside?"

Tim could be seen through the open kitchen door sawing timber.

"It is."

"Married long?"

"We're not married," said Laura firmly, and at once regretted this. "We—we're partners."

"That's all right with me," said Sheila Bates. "It's the way nowadays, I know. Makes sense, really. Marriages come unstuck." She looked down the garden at Tim. "Big chap. Needs to be—into DIY on this scale. Reminds me a bit of . . ." She broke off. "Do something about the garden, will you?"

"Oh, yes. In time."

"You've got apples down there at the end. A nice Russet, I remember. I can use any you don't want."

An exchange economy, thought Laura, when Sheila Bates had—eventually—left. Fair enough.

She told Tim about their neighbor.

"So long as barter doesn't include me fixing her plumbing."

"Come on, we should be neighborly."

Autumn segued into winter; he had the heating up and running, and basic remedial work done on the kitchen. He was sanding floors now—dust everywhere.

She had never known him so absorbed in a new project—immersed in it each evening, every weekend. It was as though he were possessed. He sanded, he replaced rotten floorboards, in fine weather he got up on the roof and started to tackle the slipped and broken tiles. He set about the creation of the en suite bathroom next to their bedroom to replace the original dank facility at the end of the landing.

Winter now in full control. Icy mornings. Snow that came, melted, lay around as slush. The house could not be called warm, despite the radiators, the state-of-the-art boiler.

Intermittently warm. She said, "The heating works in an odd way, have you noticed? There are cold patches. Here and there."

He grunted, dismissive, short with her. "It's fine. Just that the house has been empty."

He could be like that these days.

Laura cooked a lot, surprising herself. She had always been a rather lazy cook, favoring easy things, short cuts; now she found herself making hefty stews, doing complex bakery. And it passed the time—her rather solitary time; there is only so much tea and coffee you can supply.

She went for walks, too—not that the neighborhood came up with much by way of an interesting route. Too built up. On one of these she met Sheila Bates, heading for her house, dragging a shopping trolley.

"How's he doing, then? Got your heating in?"

"He has," said Laura. "He's got masses done."

Sheila parked her trolley, nodded. This was not to be a fleeting exchange, it would seem. "You know, it's maybe as well you've not got children. There was a child fell down those stairs. Wasn't all right after. The family left quite soon."

"They are quite steep, I suppose," said Laura. Right, let's have *all* the bad news.

"Ages ago. In my parents' time. There's been people since, several lots, but no children, I think. You hadn't Russets to spare, then?"

Oh, heavens—the apples. I forgot entirely. Black, black mark. "Do you know—there weren't that many. A bad year, perhaps. I'm sorry. But . . . but can I bring you a cake next weekend? I always bake then."

Sheila Bates looked interested. "Into cooking, are you? That's unusual, with younger people, I've noticed. It's all takeaway and that. All right, then. I won't say no."

There had not been much intercourse with other neighbors. A couple at the end of Sheila's terrace occasionally passed the time of day, a few faces had become familiar. Sheila seemed vaguely to be valued, as some kind of tether to this place.

Actually, Laura thought, I'm not at all sure I'd want to stay here. Something . . . oh, I don't know, something not right. Well, staying put is not likely to happen, with Tim's track record.

Sheila was saying something about the house, their house. ". . . new back then. Not far off new. Built just before the war."

"Sorry? Oh, our house. Yes, I suppose. To me it feels old."

"Well, it's not been cared for, has it? My parents never liked it."

"I must get back," said Laura briskly. "Tim will be wanting his tea." And what does it matter whether your parents liked it or not? They didn't live there. "I'll remember the cake, next weekend."

Laura found Tim sitting in the kitchen, in a state of exasperation because the wrong tiles had been delivered. She tried to cheer him up with an embellished account of Sheila Bates—the archetypal crusty old neighbor—and merely provoked irritation.

"Look—without those tiles I'm set right back this weekend. Can't get ahead with the bathroom."

"So? There's no deadline. So it takes a bit longer . . . You know, you're a bit obsessive, this time. This house . . . I don't know . . . it seems to consume you."

No reply. He was examining his plan of the bathroom, and did not look at her.

"I watch telly on my own every evening," she said.

"For Christ's sake, Laura, stop being so pathetic." He stood up, and slammed out of the room.

Later, he had calmed down, appeared to have forgotten the exchange. She was relieved, but disturbed. What was this? Tim, who was always so agreeable? Never a cross word.

At Christmas, her mother came to stay, a visit proposed by Laura with the notion that some kind of family Christmas would tame the disheveled house, normalize it. Her father had died a couple of years before and her mother, Susan Harper, was glad to come. She was gallant about the various deficiencies: "No, really, it's not that cold . . . I've coped with worse bathrooms, I promise you . . . The kitchen's going to be lovely eventually, I can see." There was a frenzy of cooking: the full-scale Christmas dinner, Laura made an iced cake, Susan an array of mince pies. The house smelled rich, seemed to mellow.

"Really warm now," said Susan. "Mostly, anyway. Just chilly places. Draughts, is it? Feels like that. Does Tim need to do something with the windows?"

"Nothing wrong with the windows," he snapped. Tense, annoyed. Busy with his clipboard, the squared paper. Susan fell silent, abashed. They had got on fine, in the past. She said as much to Laura.

"He can be tetchy, these days. Sorry."

Susan took herself off to the shops, being tactful, perhaps, on the pretext of some need. Tim was now tiling in the bathroom. Laura brought him coffee, stood for a moment. "You did rather squash my mum, you know."

He said nothing, intent upon placing a tile. Then he turned, looked at her. A look of pure hostility, that shocked her. She went downstairs, so fast that at one point she nearly tripped, her stomach lurching.

Susan returned from her excursion, with a placatory bottle of wine. She and Laura had tea in the kitchen, Tim still immersed in bathroom fittings overhead.

"I was pounced on by one of your neighbors—saw me leaving the house. Old. Asks questions."

Laura pulled a face. "I know. Her. Yes, she does."

"Checking me out. Then—how was Tim getting on? Saw him up on the roof, hopes he takes care, you don't want another accident. Went on and on . . . funny place, that, nobody stays that long, wonders why you two wanted it . . ."

"Accident?"

"Oh, someone's wife—way back when old Mrs. Thing was a child. She didn't elaborate. Offered to walk me to the shops, but I escaped."

"I'm in the market for a different neighbor," said Laura. "No one's come forward so far."

She made a curry with the remains of the turkey. Tim drank most of the wine, opened another bottle, became more congenial. They made love that night. No, Laura thought, after—we had sex. Love wasn't what we were making. He had been cursory, rather rough. He felt, indeed, almost unfamiliar, as though a stranger took over the bed.

On the day that Laura's mother left she said, "Will you actually live in this house?"

Laura laughed. "You mean, unlike Tim's other projects? Maybe. Maybe not."

"Would you like to?"

There was a silence. Laura's mother became brisk. "We'd better get going, if you're going to run me to the station."

In the car, she said, "If you really don't like the house, when he's done, you must say, Laura."

Laura sighed. "Of course I would, Mum."

After Christmas, it got a bit warmer. Tim was doing some decorating now, in the new bathroom and elsewhere. The heating seemed to have become more effective lately, and Laura would leave an upstairs window open for a while to clear the smell of paint. The Christmas break had given Tim a spell of concentrated work on the house but it was now back to routine—the daily stint at their jobs for both of them. For Laura, this was something of a relief. At least she had company, at work. Conversation. Laughter.

Everything *we* used to have. Before we came here.

Thoughts fermented, on those winter evenings, cleaning up after supper in the kitchen, watching television later. On one of those nights, restless and suddenly resentful, she took him up a mug of coffee. He was in the spare bedroom, plastering a wall.

"I suppose I can't persuade you to join me for *Have I Got News For You?*"

He did not look at her. "No. I've gone off it, anyway."

"You used to love it. *We* did."

He glanced at her. "You seem to assume that everything always stays the same." Exasperation in his voice.

She left the room, slamming the door. Ran down the stairs.

Halfway down, she felt it. A hand on her back. Between the shoulder blades. Pushing. A sharp push. Then it was gone. She had clutched the banister.

She looked back up the stairs. The door she had slammed was still shut, Tim inside that room. It had been cold, the hand. Cold through her sweater.

A draught, of course. A chilly draught from that window on the landing—must have been left open. She went into the kitchen, got herself a glass of wine, sat down in front of the television and applied herself to a program that no longer seemed particularly entertaining.

They coexisted now, she and Tim. That was how it felt. They lived together, under the same roof, but their lives were quite separate. They ate together, in the evenings and at weekends, and there might be desultory exchanges. But we never have a conversation, she thought, we never talk. It was as though the Tim she had known for six years had retreated, subsumed into some other persona. Sometimes he was short with her; most of the time he simply paid her little attention. She began to wonder if perhaps he had depression. What are the symptoms of depression?

And she sensed changes in herself. Anxiety, instability. Well, no wonder—with Tim like this. But it was more than that; she was conscious of some deep unrest. Of wanting . . . to get away, it felt like. Get away from what? From Tim? No, no. From this place? Perhaps. She never returned from work in the evening with any sense of coming home. The surroundings seemed forever alien, a place that was not hers. And the house . . . Yes, the house too. At weekends, she found herself going out as much as possible—shopping excursions that were barely necessary.

On one of these she met Sheila Bates, not seen for some weeks.

"Your mother gone, has she?"

"Some while ago," said Laura.

"Pity. You'll miss her. We had a chat."

"So I heard."

"She was saying she didn't feel you were really settled in."

She did, did she? A bit previous of you, Mum.

"No wonder, with all that building work. I said as much. He's got going on the roof again, I saw. Up there yesterday."

"He's taking advantage of this break in the weather," said Laura. "And he's not going to fall off. You said something to my mother about an accident."

"No one ever fell off the roof, that I know of. It was a woman. Young woman."

I don't think I want to know about this, thought Laura. And that's enough neighborly exchange. "I must get on—shopping to do."

"Him that lived there before the war. I was a child so I hardly remember. Big man, like yours. And the wife had an accident. Bad accident. People didn't care for him. There was talk he'd had something to do with it. Then he went."

"A long time ago," said Laura irritably. "And nothing to do with us, is it?"

Sheila Bates shrugged. "Long time ago, that's right. Neither here nor there now, I suppose. And you'll have the place all done up to the nines before long, I don't doubt."

"Well, made habitable, at least. Anyway, I must be off."

"My mother wouldn't walk past the house. She said he'd never really left," said Sheila Bates.

Laura stared at her. Turned and walked away. She's an old bat. I really have to find myself another neighbor.

She bought some salmon for supper, a favorite of Tim's. Wine, a piece of Stilton. It was almost dark when she got back, still those raw winter afternoons, the light draining by five. Tim was up on the roof.

"Come down," she said. "You can't *see*, up there."

No answer.

"Well, be careful, then."

Soon, from the kitchen, she heard the front door slam, his feet on the stairs. He would be plastering now, on the landing.

She did things in the kitchen. A sauce for the salmon, vegetables. A salad for starters. Presently, the salmon went into the oven.

She called up the stairs. "Supper in twenty minutes—OK?"

A reply, after a moment or two. "I'd rather have it later—I'm in the middle of something."

"I've put it in the oven. It's salmon."

Plastering sounds. "I said later."

She glared up at his back. "If you wanted late supper you should have told me earlier."

No response. Then, "Just keep mine."

Laura took a breath. She ran up the stairs. Halfway up. Stopped.

"Look, Tim—I've bothered. I've taken trouble over the meal. The least you can do is eat it with me."

He paused. Noticed her, now, it seemed. Looked down at her.

"Just fuck off, would you, Laura," he said. A cold voice. A note in it she had never heard before.

She froze, there on the stair. Then she turned. And as she did so she was snatching at the banister, clinging on, almost flung off her feet.

Hand on her back. Push. Violent push.

Tim up above on the landing still, plastering.

She ran down. She grabbed her coat. She fetched her bag from the kitchen. Where's my phone? The car keys? She spun from room to room, shrugged on her coat.

She stood in the hall. "I'm going," she said.

He was watching. Up there, watching.

"I'm going, Tim."

He laughed. No, someone else laughed. Tim standing looking at her, but the laugh was someone else's.

# The Bridge

Sunday. My birthday. This is where I am. This is who I am. Alison.

And how am I? I am well. I am fit. I am in full-time employment and have been for many a year. My much-loved daughter has sent a Liberty silk scarf and her heartfelt regrets that she cannot be with me but as already explained she has a job interview first thing tomorrow morning.

She has my eyes, his height, her own disposition—thanks be. She was born into a roaring January dawn twenty-seven years ago. He was not there. He is squeamish about blood. He appeared when all was tidied up.

So I am sixty. Sixty is no big deal, it seems to me. Not if you are in good health, plenty of energy, ninety-five percent job satisfaction, still reasonable looking, size twelve, mortgage paid off and the garden makeover a triumph. Oh, that rose pergola!

When I was thirty-seven I considered killing myself. I now see that that would have been a profoundly selfish act, but I was without judgment at the time.

Twenty-three years, then, that I might not have had. What have I done with them? I have raised a daughter. I have discovered a career path that has led from jobbing secretary to planning potentate. I keep a National Park unblemished; I tell people that no, they cannot add a conservatory to their Grade II listed house, and don't even think about turning that ancient cow-byre into a new-build, or putting some holiday chalets on this scenic hillside. I have been useful, I consider.

Anything else? Well, I have achieved sixty years without

committing any public offenses except for one speeding incident. I am not much of a private offender, either—equable, on the whole, fair-minded, I like to think (the conservatory builders and cow-byre developers would not agree), my colleagues seem to find me a person they can work with, I have friends.

Complacent?

Sounds like it. A CV is complacent—has to be. So if I review the record, complacency is bound to edge in. I don't feel complacent. I know my inadequacies. I am a serial worrier. I bite my nails. I can be careless—many lost key crises and bills overlooked. I don't have nice legs and I am only an average cook.

I have allowed him to get away with too much, for too long. There. Within an apparently impregnable shell there lurks a more tender occupant. Me. Essence of Alison—a person unknown to the indignant householder who has been refused permission to adorn his stables with solar panels.

Now I shall get on with being sixty, on this fresh spring morning in an agreeable home in a West Country village. Domestic chores to be done. Some paperwork. A walk, later. Supper this evening with friends a few miles away—a short drive through this delectable landscape that I help to keep untarnished. Not a bad prospect—in fact an enviable prospect from the point of view probably of most other sixty-year-olds worldwide. Sixty in Bangladesh, Afghanistan, the Peruvian Andes, would be rather more taxing, I imagine. Had one even got there.

Expectation of life in the West is over eighty. So I have another twenty years or so, probably. Seems a long time. Older, fatter, gray hairs, hips and knees and all that, no doubt. Oh, well—I'll cope. I'm a coper.

Have had to be.

Mum dying when I was sixteen. Dad all to pieces so must sort things out for myself, get through A levels, think what to do next. Should have gone to university; felt I must get on to the job

ladder. I'm undereducated, always queasily aware of that—and I
could have sailed through a degree course. Instead—secretarial
school, business training, and one thing suggesting another,
zigzag from this opportunity to that, until I fetch up with what
I do now.

Coping. With much else running parallel. Marry him when
I am thirty. Have Ella when I am thirty-two. Have Luke.

My aberration, around then. Ran off the rails a bit.

And that day. The day.

Move down here. After a while, get this job. Not exactly all plain
sailing thereafter, but plainer than before. I am on course, Ella too
is on course—good school here for her, she grows up, does well,
leaves but has not left. Ella is bright, good-looking, kind, curious,
spends too much on shoes, drives a tad too fast, should shed this
current boyfriend, and I shall see her next weekend.

So, the record at sixty. All right, a version of the record at sixty.
I am a reasonably honest person—as honest as most. Ella would
say I pick at my mistakes, chew them over. True, I think. A way
of trying to see what happened.

He would say. I have a fair idea what he would say.

You know what happened, but you don't always see what happened. Interesting difference. When I have had a run-in with
someone hell-bent on wrecking an unspoiled village or desecrat-
ing a swath of agricultural land, I make careful notes after, sitting
in the car, eyeing the cottages or the fields, putting down just
what was said. At some later point, a subtext may shine out—I
may see and hear something not apparent at the time.

Indeed. I know that I applied for, and got, a job with the county
council down here because, I said at the time, it paid quite well
and offered prospects. I see now that down here was also as far
as possible from over there, from a particular place.

I know that I have always had a resistance to fiction. I don't
much care for novels. I read travel books, biography, history. I

see now that it is a distaste for invention. I can only see stories as fabrication, lies. I may be mistaken in this. Popular taste would suggest that I am.

I know that I avoid wearing red, on the grounds that it offends my coloring (pale skin, light brown hair). I see that it is also because when we were first getting together he once referred to "that strident scarf of yours." Red, it was. I took note of his criticism, back then.

I know that I married him because I was attracted to him—all right, was more than somewhat in love with him. He was entertaining, and had turned up. I see now that I was also helplessly, archaically, panic stricken, at thirty: should marry, should settle.

He has forgotten my birthday, I note.

*

Never again costume drama. One thing after another, today: trouble with lighting in that B List stately home that costs an arm and a leg each week of filming. Commotion over costumes. Get that car out of shot. There's a phone cable there, you idiot. Give me cops and robbers any day. Or a nice straightforward sitcom.

And now this hotel where the restaurant slams its doors at nine, so it's room service or nothing.

Come on, Barry, enough whingeing. This is a diary. Get down days in the life of Barry H. Get down life as a director. Get down life.

What's the date? Oh, Christ, it's her birthday. Does room service do flowers? This will be marked down and held against me. Along with much else.

Happy birthday, Alison. Sorry, sorry. Much of the last thirty years spent saying sorry, come to think of it. Apologizing for being myself, by and large, which is a bit odd, considering that she presumably married me for myself, as it were. Married me for being what she perceived me as, when we first started going out.

Which we didn't. You didn't go out with someone back then. You saw them: X and Y are seeing each other, B is seeing this new man. If things went well you saw a great deal of her. You saw her all over, breasts to bum.

Nice breasts, she had.

The chef's lasagna and a bottle of red—that's better. Thank you, room service. I should be studying tomorrow's script, but I'm not going to. Period claptrap.

She must be sixty. Christ. Which makes me fifty-seven, something I prefer not to dwell on. My CV knocks off a few years. I play down, like aging actors. I'm usually the oldest person on the set, bar the occasional grande dame doing the dowager part. We've got one on this gig—Victorian matriarch.

Alison played down, at thirty. I didn't realize she was that, at first. And hadn't really intended more than a fling, until somehow we were apparently serious. I was that much younger and not all that set on marriage, but prepared to oblige if she was so keen. Why not? one thought. Michael rather fancied her, I'd noticed, and you always want to steal a march on your brother.

My brother the barrister. Trust Michael to have it all worked out from about age ten—copper-bottomed career. We're not much in touch these days. Hardly surprising, really.

And I, of course, have no pension, and the career is a stop-go affair—no work, spasmodic work, lucky break and zoom ahead: Advance to Go, bank error in your favor, collect £200. Scriptwriting, directing, ideas man—ask me and I'll do it. Professional enabler of stories (except period rubbish like this). I love stories. So much more satisfying than real life. Real life goes on and on, plotless and pointless. A story has form and content, beginning and end, significance.

Which my own, of course, does not. A beginning, an inevitable end. Various climactic points in between, but show me the form, let alone the significance. Our hero contrives, year-by-year, decade-by-decade, contrives himself into this and out of that, any continuous progress foiled by circumstance. Someone else beats me to that ideal job. They pull the plug on the sitcom. My script is binned. Go back three spaces. Go to Jail. Move directly to Jail. Go back to Old Kent Road. Where's the shape, the meaning? No script editor would look at it twice.

Alison would say. Oh, I know all too well what Alison would say. That I don't plan. That I don't calculate. And that I've chosen a hand-to-mouth, footloose sort of business. Unlike her.

I'll have to compensate for the birthday boob. Take her out for a nice dinner next time I get down there. Which might be rather soon. Nothing lined up so far after this job, which will mean a fallow period, and a taste of West Country life. And married life.

Can't afford the London flat anymore. Not at the moment. Maybe at some point, if there's an Advance to Go.

Hand-to-mouth, footloose. Also—flexible, invigorating, challenging. Intriguing, exciting. I have not seen the inside of an office in my life. I juggle workmates, friends. When you land up with a turkey, like this current enterprise—well, you always know there's an end in sight. Three more weeks, on this one.

Don't mind where I am—can function anywhere. Don't need a home, as such. Don't need a base, I was going to say, but that's not quite true. Fact is, she serves as a base. Sort of base. There— I'm admitting it.

There's what you admit, and there's what you don't admit. I admit that I have a short fuse, that I am leery about going to the dentist, that I am needle shy, and have been known to pass out at the sight of roadkill. I admit that I am susceptible to women, that I have occasionally fiddled my expenses, that my credit rating is poor, that I could lose a bit of weight. I admit that my spelling is erratic, that I have never read *Wuthering Heights* or seen a production of *Hamlet*, that I can't mend a fuse or change a tire, that if I have to sing I am out of tune.

This list is getting rather long.

One more. I admit that I have never had a good relationship with my daughter. Ella.

I don't admit that I am lecherous, violent, criminal. Could not do so because I am none of these things, just averagely deficient. Not a philistine either—just averse to cultural clichés.

So . . . Life as Barry H. Roughly speaking, leaving out much. The script editor in me says—come on, where's the narrative? All right, so there's no shape, no significance, but you've been round the block, haven't you? Had your moments, your days to remember.

Oh, yes. One, anyway. Day you would rather not remember. Let's not go there.

Chef's lasagna was indifferent. The bottle of red is going down nicely. Tell you what—I'll give her a ring. Alison. Say happy birthday.

Not there. "If you would like to leave a message . . ." Out on the razzle, if such a thing is possible in the depths of the West Country. And Alison has never razzled. But evidently the birthday is being celebrated, which is good. That may mitigate my own offense.

Ella? Call Ella? Not something I much do. And not at ten o'clock at night after a few glasses of red—she'd spot that at once. No, pack it in, Barry. Fold up this particularly insignificant day and put it away.

★

I haven't told my mother about you yet, by the way. Saving you up as a treat. She never cared for my ex so she'll welcome you.

Inspection? Oh yes, inspection at some point. But it's too far for a weekend and I can't start taking days off yet—I was lucky enough getting this job as it is. I may have to keep you on a back burner for some time, as far as she's concerned. Yours are easy—a short hop on the Metropolitan Line. Did I do all right, on Sunday?

She does? Ooh—that's made my day! Lovely manners . . . wait till I can tell my mum. She'll take it as a personal compliment—entirely her doing.

Don't I? Talk about him. My dad. No, I suppose I don't. Actually, my dad has never much liked me. Do you know—I've not really said that to anyone before. I feel all funny, saying it.

Oh, if I knew *why* . . . I don't think I was a particularly horrible child. Maybe he just didn't like children. And there was only me, after Luke died.

Two. Around two, he was. Couple of years younger than me. Awful for them. And of course my dad always was away a lot, doing what he did. I mean, they couldn't have been more different—Mum all focused and applied and him skipping from one project to another, in and out of work, gone for weeks and then back home chewing his nails and taking handouts from Mum.

Hang on—no *way* would I inquire after your career prospects when I've only known you for, what, eight weeks and anyway . . .

Nine, is it?

Anyway, in fact I would think in a marriage it's no bad thing for people to be in quite different kinds of work. No, with them, it wasn't the work thing, it was more they were—well, never really on the same page. Were? Are. Why do I keep saying were?—they're still married. Though I sometimes wonder why. And I've never said *that* to anyone before. What's going on, that I keep saying stuff to you I haven't said to other people?

Oh . . . Yes, I sort of feel that too.

I mean, they are so not like *your* parents. But there they are, still married. It's as though there was some sort of umbilical cord they can't shed—quite the wrong term but you know what I mean. Something that holds them together when nothing much else does.

Me? Oh, no. No, no. I'm sort of incidental, I think—though not to my mum. No, it's not me. Anyway, you've had enough of them, I don't know what started me off on this . . . Oh, not telling Mum about you just yet.

★

Ella sounds cheerful these days. This new job working out well, I imagine. And I don't seem to be hearing that Sam mentioned.

Barry coming next week, apparently: "Thought I'd take a break for a bit, and head west, if that's OK with you." I know what that means—he hasn't got any work lined up, and nothing in prospect. All right. It's as OK as it ever has been. No more, no less.

For a bit. Yes, for a bit can be quite—well, quite companionable. And . . . there's what we never talk about. It's as though being together now and then keeps it alive. All of it. What we still need, and what we could do without, that hangs there, always.

Oh, well. So I e-mail back: "Fine. See you, then."

I'll be busy, anyway. He can make himself useful, come to think of it—clean the gutters for me, paint the front gate. Never a homemaker, Barry, but it won't hurt him to apply himself to mine. Earn his keep, to put it really meanly.

Way back, way back at the beginning, there was some home-making. Combined homemaking. The little house in Highgate that we could barely afford—me with starter job and Barry getting that lucrative sitcom series, and then nothing for a while—how it would always be for him. But home was made: the kilim rug he gave me one Christmas, the Hockney print we chose together, the William Morris Willow Bough curtains I made, the blue and white junk shop china we collected.

The children.

I've still got the kilim, the Hockney, the china. Curtains left behind. Along with much else: the way we were then, the way I felt then, the way no doubt that he felt then.

Some of my friends and acquaintances down here don't realize I'm married. There have even been people trying to do a bit of matchmaking, rather touchingly: "Alison shouldn't be on her own . . ." An amiable widowed vet has been offered, and a divorced solicitor, at a somewhat obviously constructed supper party. Well, that would give Barry his comeuppance, wouldn't it? "I have to tell you that my affections are otherwise engaged."

Unlikely.

Maybe I should flourish Barry while he's here. Have people in, take him about. The immediate neighbors have seen him before, and probably think I have a fancy man who visits from time to time. I can't be bothered with explanations.

No, I shall carry on with my life as usual, and Barry will hunker down in the house, watching a lot of television, making a lot of phone calls, checking his e-mails every hour or so. And in due course, after a week, two weeks, a few weeks, he will announce that he is off. We will eat a meal together in the evenings, chat a bit. We will have the occasional spat. We will never, ever, talk about then, back then.

He had to give up the London flat, so this is now his only base. Pretty tenuous base—my spare room, in which he keeps a few things. I have other visitors so he is not allowed to take over. I can't imagine living like that—perching in someone else's house. He has never considered this one in any way his (well, it isn't), and behaves always like a guest with perhaps certain rights of occupation.

What rights?

I have never said: don't come.

Enough of Barry. I am busy, busy. My colleague is away so there are extra visits to be made, a backlog of paperwork. This incomparable landscape lies out there, requiring constant vigilance—peppered with Grade II listed buildings, rich in unspoiled scenery, and full of people poised to make a quick buck out of it or indulge their lust to interfere with what should be left undefiled.

Ninety-five percent job satisfaction. The errant five percent is accounted for by the siting of my office window, too close to a main road. Relatively meager dissatisfaction, one might say.

Life satisfaction? Let's not go there. No, let's take a peek. On the credit side: Ella. This house, entirely mine and entirely earned by my own hard work. The job, of course. Friends. Knowing I have made the best of things. The new herb garden, the green jacket I got last month, the fact that I have had that wisdom tooth out. Oh, come on—this is getting silly.

Debit? Oh, plenty. Knowing I have turned a blind eye to Barry's various infidelities. Knowing . . . knowing I once made a stupid mistake. That I am sixty. That I have varicose veins. That there is rising damp in the utility room.

That there is only Ella.

I said, let's not go there. So go no further.

\*

Go west, young man. Middle-aged man, in my case. A spell of all that dinky greenery, looking like those pre-war Shell advertisement posters, of Alison's spare room (please, love, could there be a new mattress at some point?), of internet searches, DVDs in the afternoon, early nights. Oh well, a fallow period is often no bad thing—relax, unwind, polish the creative faculties. Work up some ideas. Chase up some old contacts. Check up on who is doing what.

See Alison.

Don't see much of her now, in that sense. Fully clad only. We haven't slept together for years. By mutual agreement. Tacit agreement. No dramatic renunciation. Just, we stopped.

Her house. Very Alison—everything just so. Color co-ordinated, good taste all over the place, striking pictures, warm, comfortable. Here and there a whiff of the past—something that says: remember? That Hockney, a particular rug, the break-fast china.

I remember anyway—don't need things to remind me.

Remember occasionally a certain slap in the face. Her and Michael. Finding out about that. Finding out she had been hav-ing it off with my brother.

Not for long, I think. A fling. He'd always had an eye for her. But still . . .

Yes, yes, I know. I know, I know. Look, in my trade temptation is rife. Young actresses are very pretty.

Actually, remembering is odd. There are great tracts of . . . of darkness, oblivion, and then some moment of clarity. The close-up in a movie. Something said, something seen. Often quite trivial; other times not trivial at all, oh no.

Driving somewhere, Alison beside me, and she says, "I'd kill for a beefburger right now." We laugh. This is so un-Alison, and we both know it.

A ladder. Alison at the top of it, wallpapering in that Highgate house. And, looking at her, I get an idea for a sitcom about domes-tic life.

Trivial, both. But oddly clear.

And this: Ella, in a swimming pool—child Ella, frog-like arms and legs thrashing—and Alison walking backward in the water ahead, arms out, encouraging.

The bridge. Packhorse bridge, they call them. Gray stone.

Low walls. Arched above the river. Its ends sunk into projecting stone piers. Stones that jut from the river bed. Stone, stone.

Not trivial now. And so clear.

Arthouse movie stuff, memory is. Fragmented narrative, jumpy footage, much left out, allusions you've got to be sharp enough to pick up. Not the sort of thing I've ever been involved in professionally, but I can see where it's coming from. That's the inside of my own head.

Not a place where I want to spend much time. And the trouble is that at Alison's I rather do. On my own, except for her; no work pressures. A tedious mulling process goes on: inconsequential simmer of thought which tends to home in on dissatisfactions and from which surface these shards of the past—memory and what passes for thought bumping along in tandem. Makes me restless, discontented.

Right—the object of the exercise is to line up some more work. So get down to it, Barry. Make a list of old contacts to chivvy. Develop the idea for a drama-documentary on fracking. Take another look at that old comedy script—it's been the rounds but could be given a polish.

\*

We can't go to see my mum at the moment. My dad's there, apparently, and the whole package is more than I can face. But we will, when he's off again, which means when he's got some work. I feel a bit sorry for him, actually—he must be seen as pretty old, in his game, somewhat past it.

No—it's not my childhood home. Mum moved down there when I was nine or ten. Before that it was London. Bits of London bob around in my head still—somewhere green, Hampstead Heath probably, and feeding ducks on a pond, and a Christmas pantomime. You don't *remember* your childhood? Oh, come on, everyone has flashbacks. Dog bit you! Where? Well, there's no scar that I can see, but clearly it was traumatic if that's absolutely your only memory. The things I can remember aren't traumatic at all, just sort of snapshots. Not particularly interesting—just there. That was where I was once.

My brother? Luke. No, I don't remember him really. Just the vaguest impression of some small presence bumbling around and me being jealous because Mum was paying attention to him. It's memory of an emotion more than a memory of him. I'd have been three. I was four, just, when it happened.

Go to Aldeburgh for the Bank Holiday weekend? Well, why not, since we won't be going to my mum's.

*

Barry has done the gutters. I hardly had to ask. He has cut the grass. In fact, Barry seems all set to be obliging. He took me for dinner—a belated birthday celebration: "Where do we find a Michelin-starred outfit around here?" "We don't," I said. "We go to the Royal Oak." Which we did, and where we were seen by various people who know me and were clearly intrigued. The word will be out that Alison has a . . . companion.

Which, in a sense, I have. An intermittent companion. We go back a long way, don't we? That in itself is a form of companionship. Not the conventional marriage, but a kind of linked progress.

Over dinner we tiptoed into forbidden territory. Don't know how that happened—we never do, normally. Must have been the bottle of Chilean Merlot. We were talking about our ages—me being sixty, him with sixty in sight: "Oh, darling, don't remind me. Christ, I'll have to dye my hair or something—there aren't sixty-year-olds in my world."

"Thirty years," I said.

"Thirty years what?"

"'Thirty years we've had. Well, sort of had.'"

He pulled a face. He knew what I meant.

And then I said it. Heaven knows why. "We nearly didn't." And I told him how I was within an ace of suicide, that time. A few months after . . . Drove to this multistory car park, went up on the top, stood there. A long time. Then didn't.

"Christ, Alison." He put his hand over mine, awkwardly. "Well, thank goodness." He shook his head. "Not like you . . ."

"No," I said. "It wouldn't have been like me. I'm not the type. Reason prevailed, I suppose. I thought of Ella."

He nodded.

We had tiptoed far enough. We pulled back, talked quickly about something else.

But there—it was out. I had spoken of it for the first time, and to him. Next day, it lay around, both of us remembering and knowing that the other did. We were rather nice to each other. And now, a week later, it is not unremembered, but digested and silted over, a part of the general subtext of what is known, established. We are still being perfectly nice to each other, but less deliberately so.

And it wouldn't do to start bickering, anyway. His time here is finite, presumably, as always. Sooner or later he will announce that he has landed some work, and he'll be off.

What happens when, one day, there is no more work?

*

Alison dropped a bombshell. In the middle of a somewhat indifferent meal in this horsebrass-and-hunting-print country pub. Where you felt yourself eyed up by the local *haut monde*.

She had a suicidal moment. Back then. Soon after . . .

Bombshell because so not Alison. So out of character. Making you realize how she must have been, then. Making you think of things going on without her. Just me, for Ella.

Whew! One of those near-misses that life so generously serves up. The alternative existences that you glimpse. Well, I'm glad there hasn't been that one.

So, the calm waters of West Country life momentarily choppy. But we settled down. Just, both, feeling a bit differently, I suppose.

And I have sorted a computer problem for her, advised on upgrading her car, persuaded her to replace the spare room mattress, at my expense. I could see her thinking: does this mean you . . . plan to spend rather more time on it? I could feel myself thinking the same.

We have watched television together, and exchanged opinions. Alison has plenty of opinion; she has some odd aversion to story, to the very idea of something being made up, untrue. Documentary is her choice. Drama has her picking the thing apart—fair enough, criticism is healthy—but also dismissive because in the last resort she can't believe in it. She concedes that hers is a minority view: "Just as well, or a lot of people would be out of work, including you." But she says the problem for her is that it all seems so contrived, so *tidy*, so unlike life as lived. Ah, but that's just it, I tell her—the need to find order where order there is not, the search for shape, for significance. She sighs. All right, I say, never mind—let's watch Mary Beard on ancient Rome. Plenty of real life there.

I agree with her, of course. Life is a mess—a random muddle. Which is exactly why one is drawn to improving on it.

I have fiddled with this idea for a two-parter set in the Outer Hebrides—mystery with scenic accompaniment—I have considered that old comedy script, and junked it. I have made various phone calls, sent various e-mails, to no great effect. "Always good to hear from you, Barry . . . get back to you of course if . . ."

Well, it was ever thus. To the young Turks I am no doubt a superannuated hack. But to others I am an old pro with a creditable track record. So plow on—the only thing to do.

Ella called last night. Calling her mother, of course, not me. Long talk, they had, then Alison brought the phone: "Here, have a word with Ella." So I did. Words, indeed. Effort made, on both sides.

She has a problem with me. Always did. We've never got together. And it's my fault. My problem.

The story I shall never work on, of course, is my own. Ours. Alison's, hers, mine. What a shame. There it is, with shape, significance. And sacrosanct. I wouldn't go near it.

I've told Alison I'm cooking supper tonight. A salmon thing I do. So she can come back from her day of preserving this historic landscape and put her feet up. Chicken liver pâté for starters from the deli in the local market town, grapes for pudding, bottle of Sauvignon.

The local market town is a pretty one-horse place, the high street stationary because everyone knows everyone else and is stood there talking to them. Some copy here, surely, I've thought, but actually it's been done to death, from *Midsomer Murders* upward, or downward. No, get the shopping and run.

People live here. All their lives. And don't, it seems, go stir-crazy. Alison has, for a good deal of hers now. Nothing crazy about Alison, that's for sure. Relentlessly normal, and all credit to her. Ella too. Level-headed young woman, she seems to be—in so far as I can say I know her. On the phone, I suggested lunch next time I'm in London. "Great," she said. "Yes, let's do that." Neutral tone, I thought.

Four, she is, in my head—the memory image I cannot expel. Just four. Small figure up on that bridge. With Luke.

The salmon thing, and the Sauvignon, and afterward there will be a restrained tussle with Alison about whether we watch opening episode of new BBC drama series or whichever glamour-boy young academic BBC Four currently has tramping around Greek temples. Alison will win, and I shall wonder if maybe I have been in the wrong line of business. Any openings for an aging connoisseur of listed buildings in the West Country?

*

Last week I had a run-in with a London immigrant banker who has bought a sixteenth-century manor house and proposes to embellish the property with a conservatory extension, a games and cinema annex and a large swimming pool. It did occur to me that actually his outlook and aspirations were nicely in tune with the worst excesses of Tudor architectural vulgarity. Today we have planning laws to make sure that those are meticulously preserved.

Told Barry about him, who was much entertained, and in fact it is rather good to get home and unload the working day to someone. Barry is putting himself out to be . . . companionable. He has shopped, done some cooking, generally concedes TV program choice to me. We are behaving like, I assume, most married couples behave. I do not ask how long he plans to stay. He does not discuss his own day, which has been spent I suppose in pursuit of work, or brewing up ideas. His world has always been mysterious to me, and I know I'm a bit disdainful about it, can't take it entirely seriously. All that endeavor—and money—in order to invent, to fabricate. And yes—I know, I know—divert and entertain. I have a blind spot, and am well aware of it.

Nevertheless—despite our conflicting outlooks—this time together has been not uncongenial. He helps out. He has sorted the recycling box on Thursdays, cooked some surprisingly good suppers. And there was that confession of mine over dinner at the Royal Oak. Confession? Revelation, rather, I suppose. Whatever—it put down a marker, somehow. Gave us both pause for thought. That I could say it, that he now knew about it.

Ella has never known, of course.

He and Ella talked, the other night. I saw to it—put the phone in his hand. There is not enough contact between them—a strained relationship. Ella shrugs: "Well, I've never seen all that much of him, have I? Always coming and going, when I was a child. Always a bit—oh, I don't know—offhand."

Offhand? Was he? I know what she means. He was never exactly *fond* with her.

I don't want to know why but I do. There is always in his head what he thinks he saw, what he told me he saw. That day.

*

Quite a chat with my dad on the phone—he and Mum sound positively domestic, down there at hers. She didn't once complain about him. And he proposes lunch with me in town at some point.

Yes, I will. Look, I don't *mind* my dad—it's just that I've always felt a bit—well, a bit out in the cold somehow. I've often thought it would probably have been different if there'd been two of us. If Luke had been there. It would have been children then—not just a child.

No, no—he wasn't ill. He fell in a river. I don't know how. Mum doesn't talk about it, ever. Just one of those hideous accidents.

*

A whiff of some work. A murmur of interest in my fracking docudrama idea: "Get up a more detailed proposal and we'll have a think . . ." So buckle down to it, Barry. Repainting of Alison's garden shed will have to go on hold.

Trouble is, I seem to have gone right off work. Can't get up a head of steam, heart not in it—all the clichés. Influence of Alison? Am I too becoming suspicious of made-up stuff?

All this introspection, down here—that's the trouble. Oh, to hell with fancy language—too much mulling over, drilling down, staring into dark corners, hauling out things that were best left to fester. And none of that is made-up stuff. It's life as lived—as was lived.

I keep seeing Alison back then. The early days. The Highgate house, things we did together, Ella being born—whoops, help, I'm a dad. But that was fine.

It should be possible to rewind—to go back to that point, wipe what came next and start again with a different story. One that might run entirely differently, in which Alison and I live—not happily ever after, who does that?—but in which we stay together, we learn to compromise, to adapt, to rub along comfortably enough. And Ella. And Luke.

A story that never reaches a particular day. A summer day. A charming summer day in Suffolk, sun with his hat on, the green grass of June, mayflies rising and falling above this delectable little river beside which we are having a picnic. The four of us.

We have eaten. Cold chicken. Salad. Fruit. Crisps for the kids.

I read the paper. Alison has a book. Ella and Luke are pottering about, trying to catch a grasshopper.

And then . . . why? Why do we start suddenly to argue? About what? I don't know. Suffice it that things go wrong for some reason, and we become immersed in the to and fro "I did . . . ," "No, you didn't . . . " We are focused on each other, distracted, we don't notice.

We don't notice that the children are no longer pottering a few yards away.

Until I look up, look round—where are they?

Look toward the bridge, the little stone bridge that arches over the river. And there they are, they are on the low parapet, they have somehow climbed up, they are sitting there, their legs hanging above the water.

I stand up. Alison is up too, calling to them. And as I stand, I see. I am looking, as her small arm goes to his small shoulder.

And pushes.

★

There are times when I don't think of it for days, weeks. Don't see it. The day has not gone away, impossible, it is still lodged there, always, always, but it stops playing out. I am able to escape the sight and sound of it.

It will come back.

Such lovely weather, that weekend. The weekend break in Suffolk. We have been to the beach at Southwold—bucket and spade afternoon for the children. Today we explore elsewhere, picnic all packed up in the boot of the car, we find this lovely river spot. Complete with . . .

"Packhorse bridge, that is," said Barry. "From olden times and all that. Most picturesque."

I'll see it forever.

Ella complained because the crisps weren't the kind she liked best. There was a fuss, briefly.

I remember the mayflies. The sun on the mayflies—bright above the water.

I remember the man fishing on the far bank, just near the bridge.

What was the quarrel about? I've no idea, no idea at all. Had it been latent from earlier that day—some discontent brewing, ready to flare? Some small provocation? I don't know, don't know. I know just that we sat there on that sunny summer river bank and fought about something—an argument that blinded us to everything. To the day, to the children.

He said he saw first. And so there is what he thinks he saw. What he told me he saw.

But he didn't. We saw together.

I look up—see them. Oh my God, up on the parapet, they have climbed and there they sit—I am on my feet, I see her clutch his shoulder, he is slipping, she tries to pull him back. Then I see, I see . . . I see him fall. I see the fisherman throw down his rod, jump in the water. I see Barry running.

And I know now that it has always been there for him. What he thinks he saw. Despite what I have told him. Despite what the man said who jumped in.

How can something have happened twice over? One way for him, another for me?

*

You rather liked my dad? Well, stone the crows. Polar opposites, I'd have thought, him and you. Television odd-job man and rising star economist—future Governor of the Bank of England. Oh, you may laugh, but it's far from impossible. We'll see. At least, I hope it'll be we.

I can't get over how well it went. First time I've been down there with the two of them together, and it was all right. Largely thanks to you, mind. And if you like my dad, my mum *really* liked you. Purring, she was. I could see her comparing you to my ex, and poor Sam was wiped out—game, set and match.

Thank goodness there's a new mattress on the spare room bed. That's where my dad is normally, but there he was obligingly moving himself to the Put-U-Up in my mum's study. He seems to have been at hers *ages* now—no work, I suppose. One didn't like to inquire. But there he was, helping out with this and that, chopping logs for the fire, making that sticky toffee pudding—oh dear, the indigestion, but well meant, clearly. And Mum just accepting it all, unconcerned, or so it seemed.

Well, no. They can't seem like just any other older married couple to me. Too much history.

Dealing with the history? Can you deal with history? Hmmn . . . I wonder. I wouldn't know—I haven't had that much. And anyway I suppose I don't really know what theirs is. Only the surface stuff—that they haven't been all that much together, for a long time. Heaven knows what else—I'd be the last to know, I imagine. And I'll tell you another thing, my dad was going out of his way with me. Distinct attempts to make contact.

Oh, you noticed too. And do you know, I rather liked it. And my mum did too—I could sense little currents of approval. I'll almost say—*complicity*. One had this feeling they've been *talking* to each other. Well, so I should hope—I mean, they've been spending a certain amount of time together, on and off, for thirty years. But talking differently, somehow. I don't know—I just felt there'd been a bit of—oh, discussion of some kind. Something sorted, even. End of story, as it were.

What story? Well—how would I know?

# Theory of Mind

Martin is a cognitive archaeologist. His professional interest is in
how minds operated in the distant past. He is not the kind of
archaeologist who gets his hands dirty, troweling away somewhere. Martin mostly works in front of a screen, staring at
images. His subject is Paleolithic art; his thoughts, day after day,
are far away with Aurignacian culture, with Magdalenian culture, as he considers the floating forms of horses and deer and
bears and aurochs and bison, from Lascaux and Altamira and
Chauvet. His head is in a cave, metaphorically speaking, though
in fact it is in a three-bedroom semi in Walthamstow, where his
partner Harriet is downstairs preparing supper and shouting at
him that it is time to eat.

Harriet is a copy editor. She too spends much of her time in
front of a screen, putting to rights the raw version of someone's
book, adjusting punctuation, correcting spelling, rescuing the
author from semantic solecisms, reminding him or her that he or
she has already said all this back on page 130, pointing out that he
or she appears to have a kind of verbal hiccup when it comes to
the overuse of certain words.

"Supper! Martin! Come on!"

Harriet met Martin because she copy-edited his first book.
Author and copy editor do not normally meet; e-mails fly to
and fro. But in this instance there was a little party for the publication, and Harriet was invited. She had found the book
interesting and so was vaguely curious about the author. She
noticed at once that Martin was not enjoying the party at all. He

was embarrassed by it—not a party sort of man. He stood there, clutching a glass, receiving compliments on the book, and clearly wishing he were somewhere else. Harriet rather liked the look of him; not specially handsome, thin scholarly face (how can a face be scholarly? But they can, they can), thick hair flopping forward, spectacles, and, behind them, brown eyes that, she observed, had noticed her.

She introduced herself. The eyes widened.

"Oh! I'd somehow thought you'd be a much older person . . ." Confusion now. Awkward. Taking hasty reinforcing gulp from his glass. "Well . . . Thank you so much for your work."

"I enjoyed it," she said. "And I don't always."

Harriet is not drop-dead gorgeous—dear me, no. But not bad, all the same. She is not the sort of girl who sends men weak at the knees, but there have been several who wobbled a bit. She has a good figure, she has been told. Pretty mouth, it seems. Her hair functions nicely—short, dark, glossy, neat. She is not too fat, except occasionally. She buffs up well, if she makes an effort.

Over the years, there have been long- and short-term arrangements with men. The short-term ones were—well, just that. The two long-term ones involved cohabitation with all the fallout: rent, bills, shopping, washing up, bathroom habits, television preferences, his friends and your friends. And, eventually, a terminal falling out. Harriet has no great regrets. She is quite good at being on her own, but, at the moment Martin hove on the scene, she was probably a soft touch—somewhat ready for someone new, perhaps the permanent someone new.

She left the party wondering. They had talked for quite a while, until interrupted. He had seemed to be possibly enjoying himself a bit more.

And, a few days later, there was an e-mail. A faltering sort of e-mail, proposing that maybe she might, just a thought that perhaps, conceivably, it could be an idea to meet up for a meal. On Friday.

So thus it began. Over Thai chicken green curry he started to talk about the Paleolithic, about cave art, about the way in which the term art is itself an anachronism since those who created these images could not have been doing so with any understanding of the concept of art as we know it.

"The mind in the caves," he said. "Those minds . . ."

"Martin," she said. "I edited your book. I know about all that."

He put down his knife and fork, looked at her. Shook his head. "Of course you do. Sorry. I'm afraid I . . . Oh, dear. The trouble is I . . ."

"The trouble is that you're interested in what you do," she said. "Which is fine. Real trouble would be if you weren't."

Indeed, indeed. Martin is interested in his work, in the attempt to penetrate the distant past. He is interested in the Paleolithic, in the wild life of the Paleolithic, in the nascent mind of Paleolithic man. He is interested in all this sometimes to the exclusion of all else, as on this occasion when for a moment it slips his mind that the young woman with whom he is eating a meal is the same person who has been adjusting his colons and his semicolons and advising him not to use the expression "I would argue that . . ." quite so often.

However, Martin is now interested also in Harriet, as she becomes interestedly aware.

He wonders if perhaps she would like to join him for a walk on Hampstead Heath. Next week. She does so. After that he suggests a day out on the South Downs. The day is had, and Harriet counters with the proposal of a film—fresh air is getting a bit monotonous. And so there is a film, and a supper at her place, and another; Martin's interest is made evident in all the expected ways and now here they are, much later, in the three-bedroom semi in Walthamstow.

Martin comes down, arrives in the kitchen. He has that abstracted, shuttered look that means, Harriet knows, that he is still locked away in some cave, studying the outline of a horse, or wrestling with the challenge of explaining his new theory.

She waves a hand in front of his face. "Sit down. It's roast bison, with bone marrow for afters."

Martin blinks, sits, smiles wryly, vaguely. "Fish pie—great."

So how has your day been, Harriet?

Martin does not say this, so Harriet thinks it, for him. Actually Martin has never said this, that she can recall. So she tells him anyway. She tells him that she has been to one of the publishers for whom she works—Harriet is freelance—to discuss a new undertaking. She tells him that the undertaking will be a challenge because it is a work on climate change, scientific, technical, but she welcomes it: "At least I'll learn something." She does not tell him that the commissioning editor, Jim Bowles, has become quite a friend. Martin is not really into her friends. That is to say, he is perfectly agreeable if he meets up with any of them, but he tends to forget who is who and what it is they do. For himself, he has colleagues rather than friends. Her initial observation that he was not a party sort of man was correct; Martin's attitude to social occasions is that if necessary he will oblige, but all things being equal he would prefer to opt out.

But that's fine, she has thought. I didn't set up with him for his carousing potential.

So she goes out on her own, quite a lot. And that is fine. Of course it is.

Harriet tells Martin about this new piece of work: "But not for a couple of weeks or more—I'm still on the Ruskin book."

Martin tells Harriet the fish pie is excellent. He adds, thoughtfully, that the Aurignacian fish hook is proven to be perfectly viable. A colleague of his made a replica, out of bone, and tried it out in the Dordogne. He caught things. They ate them.

Harriet is intrigued by the thought of Martin hunter-gathering on the banks of the Dordogne. "When was that? Who made the fish hook?"

"Oh, ages ago. He was a German guy. Artifacts specialist."

Harriet has had to piece together Martin's past. He does not seem to be all that interested in it, himself; he may be absorbed, Martin, but he is not self-absorbed. She has established his career path, just about, and she knows that he has had a couple of girlfriends—well, sort of girlfriends—but that she is his first abiding partner.

Abiding for a couple of years now. No—nearly three. Goodness, is it really?

Martin finishes off the fish pie, appreciatively. They clear up the kitchen, together. Harriet goes into the sitting room, where she will read, or watch television. Martin returns to his study, and his screen. This is their evening, as are many others.

Sometimes Martin has evening commitments at his university. And sometimes Harriet will meet up with friends, or go to her book group. Harriet's friends are a mixed lot, but it is with other women that she is most intimate. The book group consists mainly of women, though this is fortuitous rather than deliberate. Perhaps women read more, perhaps men don't care to join book groups: discuss.

Plenty of discussion at the book group—about the book in question, about, often, much else. The book in question will have generated argument about why this character behaved thus, and whether that one was provoked by the behavior of a third, and whether or not the narrative is credible. There will be conflicting theories. And a light supper with a glass or two of wine.

Harriet enjoys the book group. As much as anything, she enjoys the glimpses it affords of other people's minds—of how they are thinking, responding, as opposed to the way in which you yourself think, respond. A conflicting attitude can make you reconsider your own. Or you may think: Idiot! She just doesn't get it, does she? Either way, there has been a salutary shuffling together of individual minds.

Living with Martin, and with his work, has made Harriet think quite a bit about minds, about what they do or do not do. She has thought about the minds in the caves, those minds that so preoccupy Martin, those unimaginably distant minds.

A mind rinsed clean of knowledge. A mind that knows nothing of time or space, that is rooted in its own here and now. A mind that has observed birth, and death, and is presumably impressed, in some way. But a mind that knows absolutely nothing about contraception or sanitation or immunization or the expanding universe or weapons of mass destruction or the law of gravity or economic determinism. Or, indeed, how to think about what this mind does not know.

I know, thinks Harriet, what I do not know. I know that I know very little, on the scale of what there is to be known. I am richly educated, in a twenty-first-century Western kind of way, so I have scratched at the foothills of knowledge. My head is stuffed, in fact, but an essential part of the stuffing is an awareness of my own ignorance. My limitations. The mind in the cave does not even know that it has limitations.

I know that I can find out. I can ask, I can listen, I can read, I can Google. I can be curious about the art of Michelangelo or the origin of species or how to set up my new Panasonic portable phone or cook Tuscan bean soup. My curiosity can be abstract, or practical.

Martin's interest in those cave minds includes speculation as to whether they were capable of something called theory of mind. He tried to explain this to Harriet once: "It's the brain's ability to empathize—for a person to conceive of an alternative point of view, that someone else may be thinking or responding differently from oneself."

"Oh, heavens," she said. "In that case I've known plenty of people without it."

He frowned: this is a frivolous response to a technical term. "If they were autistic, possibly. Otherwise, it doesn't apply."

"So did the cave people have it?" she said humbly.

"We don't know. We may never know."

In her early days with Martin, Harriet had been rather admiring of his capacity for detachment, and amused by that dismissal of bothersome things like bills that should be paid or bank statements that should be glanced at or his mother's birthday that should be remembered. Harriet found herself taking over these matters, and was aware that he was properly grateful. In those early days, the gratitude was often expressed— a quick hug, the book he was reading in bed discarded as she joined him.

Perhaps less often nowadays, but there you go. Nearly three years. A relationship sort of settles down, doesn't it?

Those other two longer-term relationships of hers had not so much settled as suffered internal combustion. So they were not comparable experiences.

Harriet had dealt with all there was to do with the acquisition of the semi in Walthamstow: the house search, the mortgage application, the removals from her flat and from his. Martin was comfortably impervious to his surroundings. So long as he had a room in which to work, anything would do. She would have liked to share the nesting process rather more, but learned that there was no point in trying to interest Martin in choice of curtains or the hanging of a picture.

Well, fine. That way, there are no disagreements.

In two years—no, nearly three—you do not so much get to know a person as discover them. You discover that weakness for *pain au chocolat*, the aversion to cats, the impressive mathematical ability, the inability to find the car keys, the preference for red wine, the horror of any formal occasion, the taste for old spaghetti westerns.

All of which adds up not to a person but to aspects of a person, and leaves out, of course, a vast amount—the seven-eighths of the iceberg, as it were, the more secretive aspects of the person that may never surface at all.

So which bits of Martin have not yet surfaced?

Harriet is copy-editing a book about John Ruskin right now. She has found this intriguing—the art, the writings, the Victorian mores. She has rather taken to Effie, Ruskin's wife—a marriage that ended in annulment. The marriage was unconsummated, and this writer, like so many others, speculates on the reason for this. It seems possible that Ruskin, who had never seen a naked girl before, had been aghast at the sight of Effie's pubic hair.

Poor Effie, thinks Harriet. For some reason, her thoughts turn to Martin at this moment. This is not a Ruskin situation; Martin has never been aghast at the sight of Harriet's pubic hair. He does not seem to have much noticed it. As indeed, she has come to realize, he fails to notice a good deal. But Martin is not Ruskin—oh, no. He has consummated. With enthusiasm, back in those early days. Off and on now. Perhaps more off than on. Well, nearly three years—obviously things would steady up, wouldn't they?

The Martin that Harriet now knows is not exactly the Martin with whom she had first embarked. That Martin was more indistinct; she had a good idea of him, but there was much infilling to be done. Today's Martin is more substantial—tastes, preferences, aversions and all, alongside, of course, the dominating tendency to be sitting at a screen considering aurochs and bison and the like and not to have noticed that it is time for supper, or way past time for bed.

A shortcoming that it is easy to live with, she thinks. My goodness—others have to endure infidelity, or alcoholism, or domestic violence. A degree of inattention is nothing to complain about. Some might appreciate it. You wouldn't want a man who was looking over your shoulder all the time, would you?

Harriet's friends sometimes ask after Martin, since they don't often come across him. As though to check up. And Harriet will establish him: he is working on such and such, he is off to a conference in Washington. She has outlined him, as it were, for Jim Bowles, this work acquaintance who seems to be becoming a friend. A new friend is always welcome. Harriet is reasonably well equipped, but can always find room. Essential ballast, friends, when you live with a person who doesn't care to socialize, and who doesn't much converse . . . No, that's not fair—Martin converses. But he converses rather on his own terms. If the matter in hand engages him, if he began the conversation.

Conversation, consummation, thinks Harriet. More off than on? Oh, stop this.

Sometimes, Harriet wonders about having a child. She is thirty-four. It is not yet a question of now or never. But getting that way. Once, she had wondered in the direction of Martin. Hinted. Floated the idea. Martin had not reacted. Harriet's wonder—her hint, her float—had not reached him, apparently.

So it would seem that he himself is not wondering.

And there is work, for both of them. And the daily, weekly, monthly, slippage of time. Harriet finishes copy-editing the Ruskin book, moves on to this new project, which is indeed quite demanding. Martin is . . . What is Martin doing? She asks him, over another kitchen supper.

He is assessing the incidence of portable art in eastern European cave sites, he tells her. The keynote talk for an impending conference.

Portable art? Oh yes, those deer and bears and things they carved on small pieces of bone. Nobody knows quite why. The minds in the caves at work.

When and where the conference?

Vienna, he says. In a couple of months' time.

Harriet has never accompanied Martin on any of these professional trips. He has not suggested it. Others, she has gathered, do sometimes take along wives and partners. Like footballers, she thinks—the glossy cohort of WAGs. Except that academic WAGs would not be like that at all, they would quite likely be academics themselves, and some of them would be men. Dowdy rather than glossy, and quite without any shopping inclinations.

Harriet would not want to go, in any case. She doesn't mind being on her own for a few days, or, indeed, for the occasional longer periods when Martin goes off for a serious encounter with some cave. She has occasionally taken the opportunity for a jaunt with friends.

But at the moment she is immersed in the complexities of climate change, with this new commission. Jim Bowles has been in touch, concerned that all goes well: the author in question is known to be tricky to work with. They have met up for a drink, with business not on the agenda.

If Harriet is late in, of an evening, Martin does not seem to notice. She may find that he has drifted down to the kitchen and is making himself an omelet. He neither complains nor inquires.

Over this time she is late in on several occasions.

She is late in, she is distracted, her mind is not on the things to which it is usually applied: work, remember to pay the council tax, remember to get stem ginger and kaffir lime leaves, phone Mum, get cash, go to the gym. It seems to her that this new, distracted mind must be visible, swirling above her head like a thought bubble. Martin must surely see it. He has been talking and she has not heard a word he said; he has not noticed. She stares out of the window—and she is not a person who sits and stares; he comes into the room at that moment and she has gone on staring, but he just rummages around for the book he was after, and goes out again. Harriet's thought bubble is invisible, it seems.

Theory of mind. So much for that, she thinks. My mind is churning away, it is loud, conspicuous, but Martin is quite unaware. My wildly unstable point of view is not apparent to him.

Which is, of course, just as well. She is going to be late home again tomorrow, and does not need to explain.

She feels guilty. Of course. She is taking advantage of . . . Of what? Of Martin's capacity for inattention. Of Martin's ability to be elsewhere. Her thought bubble, in her mind's eye, has a sour yellow tinge of guilt.

But it is also a euphoric thought bubble. It is full of surprise, of wonder. How can this have happened? Whatever it is that has happened.

And must not happen. Cannot happen.

How does someone morph from a man you have been talking to about a work commission to the person who fills your mind, the person you must see, the person you ache to see? How can a face that was neutral become the face that makes the blood run quicker, the face that lights up that pub, the sushi place, the Italian restaurant, the bar at St. Pancras, that walk along the Embankment?

How can I, thinks Harriet, turn from a woman who was moving peaceably enough from day to day to one who can't sleep properly, who is forever in a state of anticipation or recollection? Who stares out of the window when working, doesn't listen to what people are saying, checks her phone every ten minutes?

Harriet knows that Jim Bowles is like this, too. Theory of mind is operative here. She knows what he is feeling, thinking; he doesn't have to tell her. She sees it in his eyes: at that pub, the sushi place, the Italian restaurant . . .

Jim Bowles is not a bit like Martin. He is expansive, he is talkative, he talks about books he is publishing, books he would like to publish, books that someone ought to be writing. He is convivial, gregarious, he likes to get out and about. He is prepared to get interested in anything. He is fervently interested in Harriet and is trying—pathetically—to play this down. He knows that Harriet lives with Martin. He knows that this is going nowhere, should go nowhere.

Jim Bowles is not with anyone. He once was married—he was until last year. He has a little girl of five, who stays with him every other weekend.

Harriet goes with Jim and the little girl to the zoo. It has come to this. Martin is at the university, where there is a weekend colloquium, so she has no need of explanation. Harriet is entranced with the little girl, Lucy. I want one, she thinks, I want one. Even, I want this one.

This may be going nowhere, but it goes on. Whatever it is has become inescapable now, a fact of life, a fact of Harriet's life, of Jim's. Harriet feels that she is two people: ordinary, workaday Harriet at home in Walthamstow, and the other Harriet, who is quite often not at home, and absentminded when she is.

She came in quite lateish one evening, and found Martin in the sitting room. Not up in his office.

He smiled at her. A smile that was reserved, friendly, almost complicit. "Had a nice time?" he said.

She couldn't remember where she was supposed to have been. The book group? A film with Emma?

Yes. Thanks. A very nice time.

Harriet's thought bubble filled the room, it seemed to her. The sour, yellow, guilty thought bubble. They went upstairs to bed and it trailed up there with them. She prayed that Martin would not want to make love. He didn't.

The time came for that conference of Martin's. In Vienna. Where he would deliver his keynote talk on portable art in eastern European cave sites. He would be away for a week.

It was inevitable. Inevitable that Harriet should have told Jim Bowles this. Inevitable that when she did so they would have stared at each other in that pub, the sushi place, the Italian restaurant, wherever it was, and thought . . . thought the same thing.

They went to Lyme Regis. Chosen for no particular reason except that Jim had once published a book on Mary Anning, and had always thought he'd like to go there, and that a weekend of illicit love seems somehow to require the sea. They walked on Charmouth beach, they walked along the Undercliff. They ate fish and chips on the front.

They lay in a warmly friendly B and B that assumed them to be a couple, which was both disturbing and exciting. They lay in bed, sated, together, content. Harriet's thought bubble was not around, whisked away by one of those crying seagulls beyond the window. Jim Bowles lay staring up at the ceiling, holding Harriet's hand. He spoke of Lucy. He said he had always hoped for another child.

That did it. That did it for Harriet, once and for all.

Back in London, in the sushi place, she said: "I'm going to tell him next week. I tried last night, and then just couldn't. Next week, definitely."

"I'll tell him tomorrow," she said. In the Italian restaurant.

"I love you," Jim said. In bed in his flat, early one evening. He has said this before, and will say it again. Harriet had not heard this for so long.

"At the weekend," she said. On the Embankment. "At the weekend I'll tell him. Oh God, I don't want to have to do this."

"It's going to be such a shock to him," she said. In the Starbucks round the corner from Jim's office.

"I feel so bloody awful about it," said Jim Bowles. On the westbound Circle Line platform at King's Cross. "Doing this to someone."

And so, at last, Harriet forced herself to the point. Forced herself to honesty. Forced herself to say to Martin, as they sat at the kitchen table, supper eaten, an evening ahead: "Martin, there's something I've got to tell you."

A smile. That slightly odd smile she has seen once before. "I know."

"No," she said. "No, you don't . . ." He thinks I'll say I want to move house, that I want us to have a holiday, that, no, no . . . that I'm pregnant.

"You're going," he said. Not smiling now. Just a level look across the table. Not questioning, either.

She could not speak.

"There's someone else," said Martin. "Has been for some time."

No smile now. And a look she has never seen before. A different Martin.

She sat there. Wincing, cringing. How? But he never . . . Martin doesn't notice . . . "I didn't think . . . ," she said. "I had no idea you . . ."

"No. I know you didn't." A sort of sigh. And that look—a Martin she has not known who has surfaced and whose eyes meet hers. Eyes in which she sees—oh no, no—sorrow, regret. "Of course I knew. You weren't the same. You became different."

He is not accusing. He is not reproachful. He is just stating a fact. He is making a statement about . . . theory of mind.

# The Third Wife

They were viewing this house she fancied. He was quite happy with that. She would be paying for it anyway, and if she wanted to upgrade that was fine with him. Molly was his third wife, and had plenty of dosh—inherited from her parents, in her case. The other two had also been well bolstered—he'd always been careful to check that out. Sandra had had a business that was going great guns—designer children's clothes—and Louise had had a job in the City that paid a wad, annual bonuses and all that.

Molly had already had a look at this house—came back enthusing. It was substantial, Edwardian. Isolated, down its own drive, no near neighbors. Fine—one doesn't want rampaging children within earshot. Plenty of rooms. Secluded one at the end of a passage which would do nicely for his office.

Not that one was planning to be here for all that long. What Molly didn't know was that her days were numbered, as his wife. About a couple of months or so, when he'd sorted out some stuff with the bank accounts. Five years, she'd had, and that was just about his limit. Much the same with the others.

How do you dispose of a wife who is now surplus to requirements?

Murder?

Oh, dear me, no. Far too untidy. Far too open to repercussions. Too banal, frankly. Only an idiot would take that risk. No, no.

Divorce?

Divorce is for the unimaginative. Divorce is for self-destructive fools who want to lose half their house and half their income and half their capital and prop up the legal profession. Divorce is for those who haven't a clue how to look after themselves. Divorce is for nerds.

Oh, no. The simple thing is just to leave. Creativity is what is required.

Molly, calling from some other part of the house. "Here—come and see. The kitchen's fantastic."

He had left Sandra on a beach in Australia. Quite literally. A rather remote and deserted beach, frequented only by penguins. She had been interested in these, was dying to see them. They had driven there from the hotel where they were staying on this Antipodean holiday he had proposed as a reward for all her hard work and to celebrate a particularly good year for her business. He had organized it all—the hotel, even this beach some way away and the interesting wildlife ("I say, darling, this is right up your street—we have to go there"). He booked them in under one of his other names; it was sometimes quite a job to keep all his names sorted, and the various bank accounts. So there was Sandra, happily stretched out on a towel, sunbathing (no penguins to be seen, so far), and he got up and said, "I've left my book in the car—I'll just wander back and get it." She had murmured something, half-asleep, and off he went, taking all his stuff, leaving her the sun cream and her dark glasses and her beach bag—no need to be malevolent. There had been a couple of other cars at the parking site, so somewhere on that beach there were others, and when eventually Sandra realized that she no longer had a husband to hand, someone would take her back to the hotel, where the staff would be confronted by a hysterical woman in a bikini, whose name was not on their screen, claiming that she was staying there.

Molly, outside now. "Oh, you're going to love this garden."

Sandra hadn't known, of course, that he had cleared out much of the business before they left for the holiday. Just a matter of some creative accounting. He had said right at the start, when they were first married, "Look, let me deal with the paperwork for you. I can see to the financial stuff, all that nitty-gritty, and then you can get on with what you do so well. You shouldn't have to be bothered with the infrastructure." So the money had gone into a special account, one of his accounts. Except of course that it would only be there until he needed it, by which time he wouldn't be there either.

Sandra had been his first. He was the marrying sort. He respected marriage; he approved of marriage. If you like a woman, can see yourself set up with her, then it's the proper thing to do. The decent thing. And there was the question of funding, too, always an issue for him.

The right woman can solve the funding problem. Call it venture capital.

Molly—going upstairs now. "Four bedrooms, Stan. Two en suite."

Louise he had left in Brent Cross shopping center. In Swarovski, to be precise, where they'd been choosing his Christmas present for her, a rather pretty necklace. She was just checking a call on her mobile, and when she looked up he wasn't there anymore. He hadn't yet paid for the necklace.

He had done some interesting things with their joint bank account the day before. Really quite inventive. For a woman who spent her days moving money around the world it was surprising how little attention Louise paid to her own. She had never noticed the steady seepage from the joint account, over time. The seepage was now a hemorrhage, though he had left her enough to get through until the next salary wad from her outfit. Again, no need to be malevolent.

Molly, down again, her footsteps now somewhere at the back of the house. "Would you believe it, there's a walk-in safe! Come and see!"

There was still a bit of work to be done on the accounts, where Molly was concerned. She was no slouch, Molly—tended to be rather tiresomely attentive from time to time, wanting to take a look at the bank statements: "You're so sweet to say you'll see to all that but you mustn't feel I'm leaving it to you entirely. Money's so boring."

No, it isn't. Money is the one thing that is not boring. It is entrancing, invigorating. Motivating.

Molly was quite smart, really, though she had never had a job. Not a proper job. Well, she didn't need to, cushioned by that comfortable income from the parents who had died a while ago. She did various voluntary things now, and had a network of friends, was much on the phone. Even more so than usual, lately—he kept coming into a room where she was chatting away to someone, giggling from time to time, and would hang up as soon as he was there.

"Who was that, darling?"

"Just a girlfriend."

Susie, or Janice, or someone. He couldn't keep track of her friends. They had stolid, tedious husbands who worked in local government and suchlike, middle-management figures who said breezily: "And what's your line, Stan?" His reply was always the same: something vague about financial consultant. He had never been precise with his wives, either. They knew that he needed his home office, and had to spend a lot of time at the computer, and occasionally go away for a day or two.

"Stan, do come and see this safe."

He was Stan now, and had been since he married Molly. Before that, he had been Peter, and Mark. You did get a bit confused occasionally. And the bank accounts of course had many names; they were legion, impersonal.

"Coming," he said. "Coming."

He wasn't a big spender. Of course not. The point of money

was accumulation, not disposition. The piling up of figures, that lovely intangible hoard. His wives did the spending, and that was fine because it meant you lived very well, and it was their money anyway, not that you wanted them to be getting rid of too much of it because there was a sense also in which it was yours, or would be in due course. No, you didn't spend the money, you tended it, shifted it, made it grow. Every day he was at the computer for hours; each wife had known not to disturb him. They tiptoed around his vaguely defined occupation. Financial analyst, they said to friends. It's something like that. He's terribly clever with money.

Too right, darling.

Molly was the only one who spent time on a computer herself. The other two never did. Louise said she had enough of it at the office. Molly would be checking out clothes and stuff, no doubt, consumer research. She was quite dressy, was Molly, and always looked good. She was fun, too. But he was getting itchy feet; it was time to move on. There was a woman he'd come across at an event in London, a presentation by some fund people, sounded as though she had a nice portfolio. He needed to get to know her better; Brian, he was, to her.

"Coming, coming. Where are you?"

He made his way to the rear of the house—warren of little rooms, back here. And there was Molly, in the passage, beside a hefty-looking steel door. She seemed to be on a high today, had done herself up in a red outfit he'd never seen before, and was waiting for him there—small, sparky, really pretty, that cap of dark hair, great legs. He'd miss her, no question, but there you go.

"Look," she said, heaving open the door.

A small room, windowless, with shelves.

"What on earth's it for?"

"It's a strong room," she said. "Sort of walk-in safe. For silver,

probably. What fun! You can keep your gold ingots in here."
Laughing.

"You know perfectly well I haven't got any gold ingots." He
put his arm round her—quick hug. "So are we buying this place?"

"Shall we? What do you think?" She peered forward into the
room, switched on a light. "What's that on the shelf at the back?"

He stepped down into the room, reached forward, and saw in
his hand an envelope with his name on it, at the same moment
as the steel door clanged behind him, and he heard the click
of a lock.

Laughter again, barely audible. And he knew, began to know.
Remembered that she'd been keen to drive, had the car keys: "I
know how to find it. I told the agent there was no need for him
to come with us."

He stood there for a moment. He opened the letter.

This is for Sandra, and for Louise, and for me. I can't tell you
how long it's taken to find a house with a strong room. They've
been champing at the bit, Sandra and Louise, phoning and phoning. Incidentally, we're such good friends. I have that to thank
you for—two really lovely friendships.

Elegant, isn't it? Like your own departures. That's the idea.
Took us a while to come up with it. I wonder what you had in
mind for me?

Don't worry—you're not there forever. Depends when the
estate agent turns up with another viewer. I did make a point of
asking. This evening, I think he said. Or was it tomorrow? And
you've maybe already found there's no mobile signal. I checked
that out last week, when I had a first look. Bit of a worry, that
had been.

I wonder what you'll say? Not—my wife slammed the door
and did a runner. Oh, no. They might start asking questions, and
you'll have thought of that. No, you'll bluff it out and be

charming—that blasted door shut itself and apparently locked too, thank God you've come, if only my wife hadn't had to cry off because she had a dental crisis, and needed the car, and of course my minicab driver just dropped me off—I'd said don't wait I'll probably walk back to the bus stop when I'm through . . . You'll be out. In a while. You won't come home, of course.

Go wherever you like. They'll find you, sooner or later.

The police.

# ALSO AVAILABLE

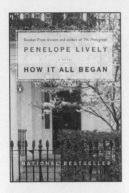

## HOW IT ALL BEGAN

When Charlotte Rainsford is accosted by a petty thief on a London street, the consequences ripple across the lives of acquaintances and strangers alike. Through a richly conceived cast of characters, *How It All Began* explores the powerful role of chance in people's lives and deftly illustrates how our paths can be altered irrevocably by someone we will never even meet.

## FAMILY ALBUM

Penelope Lively is renowned for her signature combination of silken storytelling and nuanced human insights. In *Family Album*, she masterfully peels back one family's perfect facade to reveal unsettling truths and the consequences of long-held secrets that have shaped their lives.

## THE PHOTOGRAPH

*The Photograph* opens with a snapshot: Kath, before her death, at an unknown gathering, holding hands with a man who is not her husband. The photograph is in an envelope marked "DON'T OPEN—DESTROY." But Kath's husband does not heed the warning, embarking on a journey of discovery that reveals a tight web of secrets.

PENGUIN BOOKS